The Cricket's Healing

TOON TELLEGEN

Translated from the Dutch by David Colmer
Illustrated by Annemarie Van Haeringen

PUSHKIN PRESS

Pushkin Press
Somerset House, Strand
London WC2R 1LA

Copyright © 1999 by Toon Tellegen
Original title *De genezing van de krekel*
First published in 1999 by Em. Querido's Uitgeverij, Amsterdam

English translation © David Colmer, 2026
Illustration © Annemarie van Haeringen, 2026

First published by Pushkin Press in 2026

The right of Toon Tellegen to be identified as the author of this Work has been
asserted by them in accordance with the Copyright, Designs & Patents Act 1988

ISBN 13: 978-1-80533-335-7

All rights reserved. No part of this publication may be reproduced,
stored in a retrieval system or transmitted in any form or by any
means, electronic, mechanical, photocopying, recording or otherwise,
or for the purpose of training artificial intelligence technologies or
systems without prior permission in writing from Pushkin Press

The publisher gratefully acknowledges the support
of the Dutch Foundation for Literature

**N ederlands
letterenfonds
dutch foundation
for literature**

A CIP catalogue record for this title is available from the British Library

The authorised representative in the EEA is eucomply OÜ,
Pärnu mnt. 139b-14, 11317, Tallinn, Estonia, hello@
eucompliancepartner.com, +33757690241

Designed and typeset by Tetragon, London
Printed and bound in the United Kingdom by Clays Ltd, Elcograf S.p.A.

Pushkin Press is committed to a sustainable future for our business, our readers and our
planet. This book is made from paper from forests that support responsible forestry.

www.pushkinpress.com

1 3 5 7 9 8 6 4 2

PUSHKIN PRESS

The Cricket's Healing

PRAISE FOR
The Hedgehog's Dilemma

'The spiky little mammals can never get close to each other, but this novel urges us to put away our prickles'

Sunday Times

'Those in search of a cosy, gently delivered philosophy will melt'

Financial Times

'This droll little book is cheaper than therapy'

Washington Post

'Funny and evocative, and will surely strike a chord with any social overthinker'

Breaking News

TOON TELLEGEN is one of the Netherlands' best-loved authors. A retired doctor, he initially found fame as a children's author, before beginning his hugely popular series of philosophical animal fables for adults, which examine deep questions about life and happiness through encounters between different animals. The series has sold more than a million copies in the Netherlands alone, and the books have also become international bestsellers, translated into 25 languages across the world. *The Hedgehog's Dilemma* is also available from Pushkin Press.

DAVID COLMER has won many prizes for his translations, including the IMPAC Dublin Literary Award and the Independent Foreign Fiction Prize (precursor to the International Booker Prize), both with novelist Gerbrand Bakker. He also translated Willem Frederik Hermans' *An Untouched House* and *A Guardian Angel Recalls* for Pushkin Press.

ANNEMARIE VAN HAERINGEN is an internationally renowned illustrator of picture books who lives in Amsterdam. Her books have been translated into many languages and won numerous awards.

1

It was a morning at the very start of summer. Sitting in the grass outside his front door, the cricket thought, I am content. I'm cheerful and content.

The sun was shining and small white clouds were drifting low over the horizon.

The cricket leant back, closed his eyes and quietly chirped the first tune that popped into his head.

But all at once he felt something else in his head. Something strange he'd never felt before. It was a dull feeling. And it was all through his head.

The cricket stopped chirping and pricked up his ears. It was quiet.

It doesn't make any sound, he thought. It doesn't squeak, it doesn't drone and it doesn't grate. He'd sometimes had a squeak in his head, and he'd also had droning or grating feelings somewhere behind his eyes, but he'd always been able to hear those feelings and he hadn't found them strange.

He tapped his head. 'Hello!' he said. It stayed quiet.

It's a heavy feeling, he thought. It was like his head was twice as heavy as usual. That could only be because of the feeling.

He frowned and cleared his throat. Nothing changed. He jumped up in the air a little and shook his head. Again, nothing changed. He called out, 'Oh my,' and 'Never!' and 'You bet,' but the strange feeling remained the strange feeling.

It's stuck, he thought. He sat still for a while, scratched behind his ear and looked at the sky. It's an unbudgeable feeling, he thought. That's it. He wasn't sure if unbudgeable was a real word, but it was definitely how the feeling felt.

He rested his head on his front legs. How did that feeling get into my head? he wondered.

He looked around. Maybe there were more feelings out there, skulking in the undergrowth and waiting for a chance to come flying into his head later. But he couldn't see anything special. Plus, the feeling was so big there wasn't room for any other feelings to join it. He could relax on that score at least, he thought.

He sat quietly in the grass in front of his house.

It's a big, unbudgeable feeling, he thought. If somebody comes by, I'll say, 'Hello, Squirrel or Ant or Elephant or whoever you are. I have a big, unbudgeable feeling in my head.' They would look at him and he would shrug and say, 'Oh well…'

The feeling started to press against the inside of his forehead. It wasn't a pleasant feeling. He hung his head and stared at the ground.

2

The cricket was in a very serious mood and still staring at the ground. The big, unbudgeable feeling in his head was pressing against the back of his eyes. Ow, he thought. For a long time he didn't think anything else.

Late in the morning the ant passed by. 'Hello, Cricket,' she said.

The cricket looked up and said, 'Hello, Ant. Do you know what I've got? A big, unbudgeable feeling in my head.'

The ant stopped, frowned and studied the cricket. The cricket had planned on looking up at the sky and saying 'Oh well…' but he didn't. 'I don't know what it is,' he said. 'It doesn't grate and it doesn't drone or squeak either. But it's really heavy.'

The ant walked around him a couple of times.

'Do you know much about feelings?' the cricket asked.

'Yes,' the ant said. She was convinced she knew everything about feelings, especially when they were big and unbudgeable.

'What do you think it is?' the cricket asked. A brief gleam showed in his serious eyes and for a moment the feeling seemed a little less heavy too.

'Take a few steps,' the ant said.

The cricket trudged a short distance through the tall grass in front of his door, came back and waited expectantly.

'It's a sombre feeling,' the ant said, after giving it some thought. 'You're sombre.'

'Sombre?' the cricket asked.

'Yes,' the ant said. 'Sombre.'

'But I'm cheerful!' the cricket cried.

'No,' the ant said. 'You're not cheerful. You're sombre. Because of the feeling in your head. If it was a cheerful feeling, you'd be cheerful. But it's a sombre feeling, so you're sombre.'

The sun was already high in the sky, and in the distance, at the top of the poplar, the thrush was singing.

The cricket scrunched up his eyes to try to see the feeling in his head. But he couldn't see anything.

'Anyway,' the ant said. 'I have to get going.' She said goodbye to the cricket and went into the forest.

The cricket rushed after her. 'But how is that possible?' he shouted. 'I mean—' He wanted to shout out lots more, but he didn't know what.

The ant called back over her shoulder, 'Everything's possible,' and, 'Everybody is something.' She added something about distance and today and discovering, and disappeared behind the willow.

The cricket stopped where he was and shook his head.

The strange feeling growled. But it wasn't a strange feeling any more. Now it was a sombre feeling. A big, unbudgeable, sombre feeling.

3

Actually, thought the elephant, I should climb a tree that's so small I can't fall out of it.

He was walking through the early-morning forest. There was dew on the leaves of the bushes he passed. The sun was rising.

After a while he bumped into the vole. 'Hello, Vole,' he said.

'Hello, Elephant,' said the vole.

'I've got a question for you,' the elephant said. 'You don't know of a small tree anywhere, do you?'

'I do,' the vole said. 'I happen to know a very small tree.' He jumped in the air with delight and ran on ahead. 'It's not far, Elephant,' he kept calling back. 'We'll be there in no time!'

Close to the edge of the forest there was a glade, where the vole stopped and pointed. 'Here it is,' he said.

The elephant couldn't quite see what the vole was pointing at. 'What?' he asked.

'The very small tree,' said the vole.

'I can't see anything,' the elephant said.

'It's right here…'

'I still can't see anything…'

The elephant lay down on his stomach close to the spot the vole was pointing at. Then he saw the tree too.

'Little, isn't it?' said the vole.

'Yes,' said the elephant. He'd never seen a tree this small before. It seemed like it would be very difficult to fall out of.

'So, Vole,' he said rubbing his front legs. 'Watch this.'

'All right,' said the vole, sitting down in the grass.

The elephant tried to put a foot on something and wrap his trunk around something else. But the tree was so small he couldn't do either. He spun around, wobbled, turned bright red, puffed, climbed onto his trunk a couple of times instead of the tree, and cried, 'It really is very small, Vole!'

'Take your time,' the vole said, leaning back and closing his eyes as he chewed on a blade of grass.

The elephant kept at it for a long time.

'It really is a special tree, Vole,' he said.

'Yes,' said the Vole, who was half asleep, 'very special.'

Finally the elephant seemed to succeed. 'Yes!' he said. He had put his four feet on the ground with his trunk wrapped around them and the tree somewhere in the middle. Now I just have to keep my balance, he thought.

'Help!' he cried.

'Sorry, what did you say?' the vole asked. The warm glow of the sun gliding over his face had made him think of sweet rye-cake with willow bark on a big table in the middle of the forest, and all for him.

The elephant toppled over backwards. He landed with a big thump, even though he hadn't fallen very far.

When he opened his eyes, the vole was standing in front of him.

'Small, isn't it?' said the vole.

The elephant nodded, but didn't say anything and stood up. Together they walked back through the forest.

'It could have been a little bigger,' the elephant said.

'Oh,' said the vole.

'But not much bigger.'

'No,' said the vole.

The elephant sighed. 'Trees are complicated,' he said.

The vole nodded.

'Complicated and inescapable,' the elephant said.

They reached the oak. The vole said goodbye to the elephant and carried on. He was still thinking of sweet rye-cake and inadvertently started walking faster.

The elephant stayed where he was and looked up. The sun was shining and the leaves of the oak rustled.

4

The cricket went into his house and spent a long time pacing his room.

So it's a sombre feeling, he thought. I've got a sombre feeling in my head. He would have liked to be proud of it, but he didn't feel proud, only sombre.

After a while he sat down at the table, laid his head on his arms and thought about 'sombre'. He wasn't sure exactly what it was, but he knew it was something terrible.

He tried to work out where the sombre feeling had come from. He'd never seen or heard a sombre feeling before. Maybe it comes from the desert, he thought, or somewhere else he'd never been. From the moon, perhaps.

'Do you come from the moon?' he asked in a loud voice. There was no answer.

Maybe it's an invisible feeling, he thought. But if it was invisible, how could it be heavy? That didn't seem possible.

If I could look inside my head, I'd be able to see it, he thought. Big and grey and unbudgeable.

Thoughts were shooting back and forth above and under the feeling in his head, or squeezing past it. My thoughts have been sidelined, the cricket thought. Oh, yeah? they snapped back. You've been sidelined!

The cricket flinched. Who are they really? he thought. And who am I? But just when he was trying to think these questions through, the sombre feeling lashed out hard. Showing them who's the boss, the cricket thought bitterly, and beyond that he didn't think anything else at all.

After a while, tears came to his eyes, trickled down his cheeks and fell on the table.

Now this, he thought. He felt himself growing very sad.

It was like his head was an enormous stone he had to lift up and if he didn't lift it up, it would roll down a slope.

I have to lift it up, I have to lift it up, he thought. Because he didn't know what was at the bottom of the slope.

He lay down on his bed but couldn't sleep. Instead he stared up at the ceiling and it was like the ceiling was staring back at him with big angry eyes.

The sombre feeling was pounding against the side of his head. 'You want to get out?' the cricket asked. 'Fine by me! Just say how. Through my eyes? My nose? My ears? My mouth? Exits galore!'

He closed his eyes and pictured the sombre feeling worming its way out through his ears like a mass of black sludge. Ow, he thought.

He opened his eyes again. Nothing had happened. The sombre feeling was still pounding. It doesn't want to get out at all, thought the cricket. It's pounding for some other reason. But he had no idea what that reason might be.

He got up and walked to and fro, sat back down at the table, went outside, lay down in the grass, stood up and went back inside.

You're unbudgeable, he thought. I know… He hit himself hard on the head and shouted, 'Go away!' but the only thing that happened was that he fell over, bruised his feelers and got a bump on his forehead.

The sombre feeling couldn't have cared less.

5

The sun had set and the cricket was tired. He was sitting in a chair, looking out through his window. The top of the oak rustled softly in the pale twilight and high in the air the swallow sped past.

Inside his head the sombre feeling was still unbudgeable.

The cricket fetched a jar of sweet blades of grass from the cupboard. I have to eat something, he thought. But he couldn't swallow a single blade. It's like they've all gone bad, he thought.

He shook his head. It's me who's gone bad, he thought. Not the grass. They're the tastiest blades of grass in the whole forest. No, it's me who's gone bad.

'Thanks a lot, sombre feeling in my head,' he whispered, 'for this delicious meal…'

He pondered for a moment. Maybe I'm better off not whispering things like that, he thought. Because if that feeling gets angry... Angry and sombre: my head's bound to be too small for a combination like that. It would explode.

For a second, the idea that maybe that would be best flashed through his mind before he shuddered and thought, No, I mustn't make it angry.

His stomach was empty and rumbling a little, but he couldn't eat. He put the jar of sweet blades of grass back in the cupboard, looked out of the window and saw the stars twinkling in the sky. They seemed to sting his eyes because tears started rolling down his cheeks again.

I don't want to cry! he thought. Let the sombre feeling cry, not me.

He looked back at his room.

It was now completely dark.

The cricket lay down on his bed. He was cold. But he didn't pull up the blanket. I don't know why not, he thought.

He looked at the ceiling and again it was like the ceiling was looking back at him through the darkness.

He put his pillow on top of his head. Nobody needs to see me, he thought. And definitely not my ceiling.

He lay there like that, with his head under the pillow, all night. He desperately wanted to sleep. If he'd needed to grab someone around the knees and beg them to let him sleep, he'd have grabbed them around the knees and begged. But there was nobody there. He was alone and he didn't sleep.

It all comes down to me, he thought gloomily. To me and nobody else.

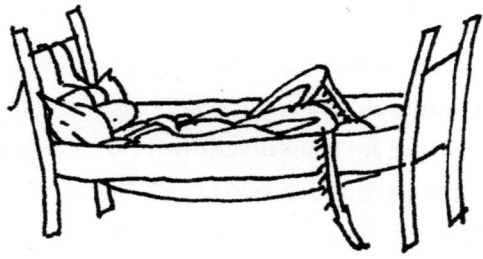

6

In the middle of the night, the cricket's door opened. The cricket was too scared to move. In the corner of his eye he saw someone coming in.

Who could that be? he thought. Could it be somebody bad, somebody who was bad through and through? He'd sometimes heard that characters like that existed, but he'd never encountered any.

After waiting for a moment, the cricket asked, 'Who are you?' His voice was hoarse.

The stranger looked around, lifted up the cricket's bed and looked under it, opened the cupboard, grabbed a jar of sugar-coated dandelions and sat down at the table.

'The gallworm,' she said. She waited for a moment, then added, 'Hello, Gallworm,' in a shrill voice.

'Hello, Gallworm,' the cricket whispered.

'That's a good boy,' the gallworm said.

It was quiet for a moment.

'I'm the cricket,' the cricket said at last.

The gallworm didn't say anything; she just finished off the jar of dandelions and went over to stand at the window and look out into the ink-black night.

The cricket had never even heard of her.

'What have you come here for?' he asked.

The gallworm cleared her throat and said, in that same shrill voice, 'Oh, wonderful, Gallworm. It's so nice, an unexpected visit like this.'

'I…' the cricket began, but didn't know what else to say.

The gallworm started singing. It was a raucous, strident song about fistfights and contempt. The lamp swung from side to side and the walls creaked.

Shall I tell her that I have a sombre feeling in my head, thought the cricket, and that it's the middle of the night? But he didn't interrupt the song.

Finally it was finished.

'Thanks very much for the applause,' the gallworm said after several seconds of deep silence. 'Thank you.'

'I…' the cricket began again.

'Dance?' asked the gallworm.

She came closer and pulled the cricket out of bed.

'I'm sombre,' the cricket said. 'I have a sombre feeling in my head.'

'As if that makes any difference,' the gallworm said.

The cricket didn't understand what she meant and the sombre feeling in his head was so heavy his legs buckled after the very first dance step.

The gallworm lifted him up and stuffed him under his bed.

'You dance beautifully, Gallworm,' she said. 'Thank you ever so much!'

Then she upended the table and chair, swept everything on the shelves out onto the floor and knocked over the cupboard. 'A little disorder is the very least I can do…' she mumbled.

Then she went to the door and looked around the room one last time.

'Thanks for your wonderful visit, Gallworm,' she shrieked, then added, 'Oh, it was nothing, Cricket…' in a deeper voice.

I'm sorry! the cricket wanted to call from under his bed. I'm sorry! But no sound came out of his throat.

The gallworm walked out and disappeared in the gloom. She left the door ajar so that the dark night wind kept banging it shut and blowing it open again.

The cricket was lying on the floor under his bed and couldn't get up.

It was a sombre visit, he thought and tried to nod to himself. If you're sombre, everything is sombre, he thought.

He closed his eyes and wrapped his front legs around his knees. His back cracked and there were drilling and sawing sounds inside his head. What are you doing in there? he thought. Never in his whole life had he felt this sad before.

7

The elephant was standing under the willow. It was early in the morning.

'I'm coming up, Willow,' he said. He put his foot on the lowest branch. But the wind rose, and the branch swung side to side and threw the elephant to the ground.

'Hey!' the elephant cried. 'I hadn't even started!'

He stood up again and curled his trunk around the tree. But the willow groaned and creaked and wrestled free.

The elephant got angry and said, 'I'm free to climb whenever I like.' But he fell again.

'I demand you let me climb!' he shouted as he got back up and brushed off the dust.

Again he put a foot on the willow's lowest branch. But again the willow resisted with all its strength.

The racket soon drew in animals from all directions. They sat down in a big circle around the willow, while the carp, the pike and the stickleback watched from the river. Only the cricket, who was still under his bed, stayed away.

Some animals were for the elephant and called, 'Come on, Elephant! You can do it!' Others were for the willow and shouted, 'Hang in there, Willow! Don't give up!'

It was a fierce struggle. The elephant took long run-ups and leapt at the willow with all four legs pointing forwards, or else he tried to pull the willow down with his trunk. The willow swished and lashed him with its branches.

Nobody knew who was going to win.

'I will climb you,' the elephant bellowed. And he also shouted, 'Make way!' and, 'Oh, yeah, Willow? Really??' The willow fought silently, but with grim determination. Now and then it groaned for a moment and dropped some weary leaves.

By the end of the morning they were both exhausted.

With a final effort, the willow wrapped its lowest branch around the elephant's middle and hurled him far away, into the river.

The animals cheered or murmured their admiration, while the carp, the pike and the stickleback quickly swam out of the way.

The elephant climbed the bank. With his head bowed, he walked through the fallen leaves and broken twigs to the willow. Water was pouring off his grey back. For a moment, he stood there. Then he patted the willow on its bark.

'You win,' he said quietly.

The willow rustled and some animals thought they could make out the words, 'Ah… it was nothing.' The willow was a friendly tree, not a mean tree.

With heavy, wet steps, the elephant trudged into the forest. Under the oak, he stopped and let out a deep sigh. The oak, who looks out over the whole forest and had seen it all, rustled its leaves.

'No,' said the elephant. 'No! No. And no again.'

He tried to keep walking, but stopped and looked up.

8

Late in the morning the cricket crawled out from under his bed, righted his table and chairs, stood his cupboard back up and put his hat and other possessions back on his shelves.

He sat down at the table and started writing.

Dear Beetle,

he wrote, then closed his eyes to think.

Suddenly he heard a loud noise and looked up. Words were forcing their way into his room. They were coming through the window, through the chinks in the walls and under the door. They were small, dressed in black coats and racing after each other. He saw 'things' and 'are' and 'fine' and 'here'. They went and stood on one side of the room.

On the other side of the room he saw 'I' and 'am' and 'very' and 'sombre', who had apparently come in through a hole in the roof. They were a little larger and dressed in slightly blacker coats.

The cricket couldn't move. Lying in front of him was the letter with *Dear Beetle* at the top.

The words stamped on the floor three times, then charged each other. In the middle of the room they grabbed hold of each other, grappled each other to the floor, kicked each other and tried to tear each other apart.

Dust swirled and the cricket coughed.

It was only much later that the dust settled and it grew quiet again. The small words had won, even though they were covered with welts and scratches and their coats were torn. The big words had lost. 'I' was broken, 'am' lay in two pieces under a chair, 'very' was folded double and hanging from a nail in the wall, and 'sombre' was crumpled and upside-down in a corner.

The small words brushed the dust off their coats, lifted up the vanquished words and threw them out of the window, where they landed on the ground with dull thuds.

'Ow,' the cricket heard someone mumble. That's bound to be 'I', he thought.

'Things', 'are', 'fine' and 'here' stayed behind in the room. They patted the cricket on the shoulder, pulled him up onto his feet, threw him up in the air and caught him again.

'Fine' climbed onto the cricket's head, 'here' perched on his back and 'things' and 'are' hung off his wings.

'Fly!' they shouted. 'Fly!'

The cricket spread his wings, rose up a little, then slumped back down on the floor.

'Oh…' the words cried in disappointment. They got down off the cricket and climbed onto the paper, under *Dear Beetle,* lining up next to each other. 'This will have to do,' they said.

The wind rose, blew in through the window, raised the letter and swept it away. 'But…' the cricket cried. It was too late. The letter was already flying through the sky.

The cricket stayed there on the floor all afternoon. The sombre feeling jumped side to side in his head and pounded against his temples, hour after hour.

At the end of the day, the wind blew a letter into his room. It fell on the floor in front of the cricket's nose.

The cricket read:

THE CRICKET'S HEALING

Dear Cricket,

Things are fine here too.

BEETLE

Then the cricket started to cry. Tears gushed down his cheeks and flowed over his wings and feelers and feet.

His shoulders jerked up and down.

It was the saddest letter he'd ever read.

9

The cricket walked to the beetle's house. It was early in the evening.

He knocked on the door.

'Yes?' said the beetle.

'It's me, the cricket,' the cricket said. 'Shall I come in?'

'Yes,' said the beetle. The cricket went into the house.

They nodded at each other then looked down at the floor.

'I wrote you that letter...' the cricket said.

'Yes,' said the beetle.

It was quiet for a moment.

'Things aren't fine with me,' the cricket said.

'No, nor with me,' said the beetle.

'I'm actually sombre, Beetle,' the cricket said.

'Me too,' said the beetle.

'I became it yesterday,' the cricket said.

'I've always been sombre,' said the beetle.

The cricket looked at him with surprise. 'Always?' he asked.

'Yes,' said the beetle.

'Haven't you ever been anything else? Like cheerful or happy?'

The beetle thought for a while.

'Once,' he said, looking past the cricket at the wall. 'There was one occasion when I was cheerful.'

'Yeah?' said the cricket.

'Yes,' said the beetle. 'I couldn't vouch for the consequences, Cricket. It was terrible.'

The cricket thought for a moment about consequences you couldn't vouch for and wondered how you were supposed to know what kind of consequences were coming.

Then he asked, 'What were you cheerful about?'

'Nothing,' the beetle said, throwing up his front legs. 'Absolutely nothing!'

'And then?'

'I've been gloomy ever since.'

Suddenly he stood up and looked at the cricket with dark eyes. He waved a fist and cried, 'I'll stay gloomy forever! Always! I promise!'

'But... that's terrible,' said the cricket.

'Yes,' the beetle said, suddenly quiet again. 'It is terrible, it's terrible too.' He sat down again. 'But it's also wise,' he said.

A little later they drank black tea in a corner of the room, far from the window. The beetle told him about all kinds of unknown aspects of sombre feelings and being sombre, and the cricket tried hard to commit them all to memory. The beetle also showed him the plates hanging on his walls: 'It's great to be gloomy'; 'There is nothing else'; 'Whatever you do, stay sombre'; and 'If you don't feel down, you're really down'. He said he read the plates every day.

It had grown dark.

The beetle said that he had given up all hope long ago. 'That was a big step, Cricket,' he said. 'But there was no getting round it.' Again he looked past the cricket at the wall. 'If you don't give up hope, you can never be completely sombre.'

The cricket told the beetle that it was time for him to be heading back home and said goodbye. The beetle nodded and mumbled something unintelligible.

Back out in the open air, the cricket felt for a moment as if his sombre feeling had disappeared. He jumped in the air and cried, 'Yes!' He pictured the beetle standing before him and imagined him clearing his throat and mumbling something gloomy. He is *so* sombre… he thought and shook his head.

But I'm sombre too, he thought immediately afterwards. His sombre feeling was as big and heavy as a boulder inside his head.

Shall I give up hope too? he thought, walking through the dark. Is it better to be completely sombre instead of just mostly?

But he didn't know how to give up hope. I should have asked him how, he thought, and shook his head.

10

The elephant was walking through the forest. The trees were rustling. Hello, trees, he thought. He knew them so well. He'd fallen out of each and every one of them.

He walked for hours, deep in thought. Now and then he bumped into a tree, but not hard. Ow, he would think, then carry on walking.

He came to a part of the forest he'd never been to before. Suddenly he saw a sign in front of a tall, thick tree:

>   NOBODY CAN FALL OUT OF THIS TREE.
>   IT'S IMPOSSIBLE.

The surprised elephant came to a halt. It was a tree he didn't know. He wanted to climb to the top right away because it was just the kind of tree he'd always hoped to find.

But he still sat down first to reread the sign. Who could have made it? he thought. How would they know it was impossible? If nobody could fall out of the tree, did that mean they could climb it? And if somebody could climb it, how would they get back down? Never, maybe?

He stood up, went over to the tree and put his foot on the lowest branch. But he didn't dare to start climbing. He didn't trust the tree.

Maybe it's not an honest tree, he thought. I don't know...

'Hello!' he called. 'Does anybody know this tree?'

Nobody answered. Nobody lived in that part of the forest.

Finally, after hesitating for a long time, the elephant climbed the tree. Otherwise I'll never find out, he thought.

He climbed very carefully, thinking about every move.

It seemed to be an ordinary tree.

Halfway up, between two branches, he saw another sign:

SEE?

The elephant was so surprised he put his foot in the wrong place, fell to one side and landed on the ground with an enormous thud.

He lay there dazed. I wasn't even at the top... he thought indignantly.

A little later he got back up onto his feet and looked up. 'Do you call that not falling?' he shouted.

The tree rustled, large and imperturbable.

The elephant rubbed his head, then made a sign to put next to the first one:

THIS IS NOT TRUE.
THE ELEPHANT (WHO FELL OUT OF THIS TREE)

Underneath he drew an arrow pointing at the first sign.

It's a dishonest tree, he thought. I hope I never see it again.

He turned his back on the tree and walked into the forest.

After a while he came to the oak. 'Hello, Oak,' he said. He knew the oak and the oak knew him.

A little later he started climbing.

The branches made friendly creaking sounds when he put his feet on them, and the leaves seem to be rustling something nice in the gentle summer breeze. Nothing is impossible, thought the elephant cheerfully. Nothing at all!

When he got to the top, he wanted to sing a duet with the oak. 'We can do that, can't we, Oak?' he asked. He also tried, while clearing his throat, to stand on one leg.

Then he fell, with a thundering crash, right through the branches and leaves.

There was nothing deceitful about this fall, and he landed on the ground with a loud thud, on a morning in summer.

11

In the middle of the forest, under the elder, not far from the beech, lived the tortoise.

One morning she was sitting in the grass under the elder and thinking about her shell. What would I do without you… she thought. She couldn't understand why everyone didn't have a shell. She found it mystifying.

The leaves of the trees rustled gently.

My shell is the most beautiful thing in the world, thought the tortoise. It's even more beautiful than the sun.

She scratched behind her ear. Is that really true? she thought.

She imagined carrying the sun on her back.

It got very hot.

Then she knew for certain that her shell was more beautiful than the sun. And also more beautiful than the deer's antlers, the carp's silver scales, the kingfisher's blue feathers and even the snail's tentacles. She thought those tentacles were fabulous. But two tentacles like that on her head... Perish the thought.

She sat there contentedly in the morning light. Later, if she'd had enough of thinking about her shell, she could always think about nothing or something very unusual, whatever popped into her head.

She heard a sound and looked up. It was the cricket trudging past. Usually he fluttered or flew, or strode past with long, elegant steps. Usually he's in a hurry, thought the tortoise. A cheerful hurry.

Now the cricket was trudging and looking down at the ground.

'Hello, Cricket,' said the tortoise.

'Hello, Tortoise,' said the cricket, looking up. He stopped in front of the tortoise, who lowered her eyes, something she never did otherwise.

'I'm sombre,' said the cricket.

'Oh,' said the tortoise.

'It's only recent,' the cricket said.

'Oh, yeah?' said the tortoise.

'Yes,' said the cricket. 'Unexpected. It's a feeling in my head. A big unbudgeable feeling.'

'Oh,' said the tortoise.

The cricket sat down. 'I'll just sit down,' he said.

'Yes,' said the tortoise.

For a long time they didn't say anything else. The tortoise was thinking about her shell again. Maybe it can block sombre feelings, she thought. But then she decided to think about something else, because she was scared that her shell might also have disadvantages that could suddenly occur to her.

'Would you like something to eat?' she asked.

'What?' asked the cricket.

'Well... um... sweet clover... or a tasty buttercup...' said the tortoise.

'No,' said the cricket, shaking his head. It was the first time he'd said no to a tasty buttercup.

Again it was quiet for a long time.

'Are you something too?' the cricket asked at last.

The tortoise was startled by the question and began pondering it.

'I'm self-contained,' she said.

'Oh,' said the cricket.

The tortoise suddenly felt very hot and flustered, but the cricket got up and trudged off again.

It wasn't until he was quite far away that he turned and said, 'Oh, yeah. Bye, Tortoise.'

'Bye, Cricket,' said the tortoise. There were small beads of sweat on her forehead because now that she'd said she was self-contained, she had to be it too. But how contained did you have to be to be self-contained?

Why am I always something I don't know understand? she thought and, turning red with shyness and embarrassment, she hid in her shell.

12

The cricket went to visit the owl, who lived in a gloomy part of the forest.

'I'm sombre, Owl,' he said.

'Yes,' said the owl, nodding her head.

'It's a feeling,' the cricket said.

The owl nodded again.

They went inside and sat down in a dusty corner of the room.

The owl showed the cricket a book about all kinds of sombre things. There were sombre suspicions, sombre birthdays, sombre excursions, sombre sugar.

The cricket saw sombre thoughts too.

'Those are my thoughts,' he said, pointing them out.

The owl nodded.

After a while he closed the book and they drank sombre tea, which the owl had made for the occasion.

The cricket let his shoulders droop and peered into the black tea.

'It's very bad,' the owl said, 'but there's something much worse.'

The cricket looked up. He hadn't known that and couldn't imagine it.

'What?' he asked.

But the owl didn't want to tell him. 'I can't say,' she said.

'Why not?' asked the cricket.

'I just can't!' the owl screeched, and stood on her head for a moment, flapping her wings.

'Sorry about that,' she said when she was back on her feet. 'Whenever I talk about it, I always have to stand on my head for a moment.' She brushed some dust off her shoulders.

The cricket peered into his tea again.

The owl pointed to a book on the top shelf of a bookcase. It was the biggest book the owl owned.

'It's in that book,' she said. 'But it's too heavy to pick up.'

'Is it much worse than sombre?' the cricket asked.

'Much worse,' said the owl. 'Much, much worse.'

They didn't say anything else and both peered into their tea.

Not much later, the cricket went back home.

Lost in thought, he walked through the forest. He was trying to think of something worse than his sombre feeling. Maybe it's like honey cake, but in reverse, he thought. When he ate honey cake it was the most delicious thing in the world. But at the same time he knew there was something much tastier, something that was always tastier. But he never knew what it was.

He stopped. That was before, he thought. Honey cake used to be the most delicious thing in the world.

He rubbed his forehead. But if there's something much worse, he then thought, maybe my sombre feeling isn't so bad.

He knocked on his head. 'Hello, Sombre Feeling,' he said. 'Maybe you're not that bad…'

The sombre feeling seemed to shrink with fright and pulled back into a distant corner.

Sunlight slid over the cricket and crept silently into his head, and he thought of a loud party and sweet honey cake and jumped in the air.

Then the sombre feeling filled his head again. He turned his gaze back to the ground and trudged on.

Not so bad is still bad, he thought. It's still really bad.

13

When the animals saw the sombre cricket trudging through the forest with downcast eyes it made them sombre too. In the bushes, the lion let out a sad roar after the cricket passed within inches of him without looking up or around.

The pike swam listlessly downstream after seeing the cricket standing above water under the willow and staring mournfully at the opposite bank.

The frog heard the cricket sighing despondently and immediately stopped croaking, while the heron, who was standing next to her, mumbled, 'I don't feel like doing anything any more…'

The elephant was just putting a foot on the lowest branch of the linden when he saw the cricket shuffling past the oak with his nose almost dragging along the ground. Dispirited, he continued climbing and didn't complain when he fell from the top of the linden.

After seeing the cricket sobbing, the butterfly could only think of crashing and fluttered on dolefully.

The bear pushed away a honey cake when he heard the cricket groaning in the distance, and the rhinoceros, who heard it too, wrote a letter to himself in which he called himself useless. That's exactly what I am, he thought, when he received the letter a little bit later. Completely useless.

The thrush looked down from the oak, saw how the cricket's shoulders were slumping, then sang the most melancholy song she had ever sung, and the weasel whimpered in the undergrowth when she caught a glimpse of the cricket.

It was a sombre day. Everyone was sombre and dejected.

But towards the end of the afternoon, everyone got used to the cricket and by early evening, nobody was sombre any more, except for the cricket.

The elephant cheerfully climbed a new tree, and the frog was croaking loudly and incessantly again, while thinking, This is so beautiful…

When somebody asked, 'Is the cricket still sombre?' somebody else said, 'Sombre? The cricket? Oh yeah, that's right.'

Some animals stopped talking about the cricket and talked about the sombre cricket instead. But in the course of the evening, they started calling him the cricket again, because they were now convinced that he'd always been sombre.

'We don't call you the slow snail either,' they said to the snail.

'No,' said the snail. 'That's true.'

Night fell, and deep in sombre thought, the cricket trudged home without anyone looking at him or thinking of him.

But when he was still sombre the next day, some animals started thinking about him again, and by the end of the afternoon, everyone was thinking about him.

14

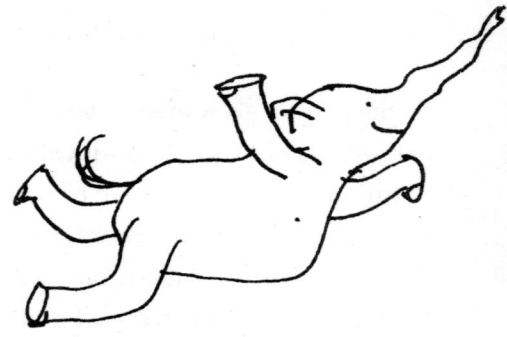

The elephant wrote a letter to all of the animals asking them to come to the glade in the forest. *As a personal favour,* he wrote.

All of the animals came except for the cricket, who was too sombre to do anyone a favour.

After they had all sat down, the elephant said, 'Dear animals, when I climb a tree I always fall out of it.'

He waited for a moment and looked around to see what the animals made of that. But the animals kept quiet and thought, Yes, when he climbs a tree he always falls out of it…

The elephant cleared his throat and continued. 'I fall because I climb,' he said.

Yes, the animals thought. That's right.

'So I shouldn't climb any more,' the elephant said. No, you shouldn't, the animals thought.

'But how else do I get to the top of the tree?' the elephant boomed and looked around with a questioning expression.

The animals racked their brains and furrowed their foreheads. But they didn't know the answer.

'I've thought long and hard about this,' the elephant said, looking at each animal in turn. Then he said, 'I know how.'

Oh, thought the animals. They were curious.

'Somebody has to throw me into a tree,' the elephant said.

'Throw you?' the surprised animals asked.

'Yes,' the elephant said.

'But who?' the animals asked.

'You,' the elephant said. 'All of you. Together.'

'Us?' the flabbergasted animals exclaimed, and they scratched the backs of their heads or under their fins and squeezed their noses in bewilderment.

But the elephant set to work immediately and showed everyone where they had to stand and what they had to do. He'd thought it all out in advance.

Soon the animals were standing packed together under the oak on the edge of the glade.

The elephant climbed on top of them. The animals reached up over their heads with their arms and wings and grabbed hold of him.

'Now lean back,' the elephant called. The animals leant back.

'Now brace yourselves,' he called. The animals braced themselves.

'Now take a deep breath.' The animals took a deep breath.

'And now throw!'

With all their strength, the animals threw the elephant at the oak.

The elephant flew through the air and slammed into the top of the tree at high speed. He was just able to wrap his trunk around the uppermost branch.

The oak swung back and almost touched the ground, but straightened up again.

The elephant stood up. 'I made it!' he shouted down.

Still panting from the effort, the animals looked up.

'See…' the elephant shouted. He tried to stand on one leg and do a small pirouette.

With an enormous din he plunged down and landed on the ground in front of the other animals.

A thick cloud of dust rose up and the elephant lay there, softly groaning.

The animals decided to go back home. 'At least we did him a favour,' they said.

Only the squirrel stayed behind. He gently helped the elephant back up onto his feet.

'So climbing's not necessary, Squirrel,' the elephant groaned.

'No,' said the squirrel.

'We know that now,' the elephant sighed.

'Yes,' said the squirrel.

'But falling's essential,' the elephant whispered.

'Yes,' said the squirrel.

'Falling is a must!' the elephant shouted in a hoarse voice.

'Yes,' said the squirrel, and he carefully patted some dust off the elephant's back.

15

When he heard that the cricket had become very sombre, the wood-mite thought, I'm never anything.

He was never cheerful, never earnest, never angry, never unfriendly and never disconsolate. As far as he knew, he had never been anything.

I'd like to become sombre too, he thought.

Early in the morning, he headed off to the cricket's. On his back he was carrying a mouldering beech branch, eating some of it now and then on the way.

Around midday, he arrived at the cricket's house.

The cricket was sitting in front of his door and staring gloomily at the ground.

'Hello, Cricket,' said the wood-mite. The cricket looked up.

'Hello, Wood-mite,' he said.

The wood-mite cleared his throat and said, 'I want to be sombre too.'

The surprised cricket stared at him.

'I'm never anything!' the wood-mite cried. 'Never!' He stamped his foot. 'Not even furious!'

The cricket nodded, but didn't say a word.

The wood-mite summed up all the things he wasn't: meek, elusive, carefree, shrewd, ingenuous, amiable, greedy, stubborn, imposing.

'I'm none of those things either,' the cricket said.

'But you are sombre,' the wood-mite said.

The cricket didn't answer.

'Not me,' said the wood-mite.

'It's something in my head,' the cricket said. 'A sombre feeling. I don't know how it got there.'

He talked about the sombre feeling and all the things it did: thumping, drilling, kicking, pounding, stabbing, scratching, grating, chafing and much more. 'It's terrible,' he said.

'But having nothing is more terrible!' the wood-mite said.

The cricket didn't answer, and they sat together in silence for a long time. The cricket didn't offer the wood-mite anything and the wood-mite couldn't think of anything else to ask about. I'll never become anything, no matter what I do, he thought.

When it got dark, the cricket went inside to lie on his bed and stare up at the ceiling.

The wood-mite walked home. In the twilight he kept looking around to see if he could catch a glimpse of a sombre feeling somewhere. When he saw one, he grabbed it and stuffed it into his head. It pounded and poked for a moment, but it was too small and shot out again. 'Nothing ever works out!' moaned the wood-mite. The sombre feeling seemed to hesitate for a moment, then disappeared into the undergrowth.

The wood-mite made it home late that night.

He sat down at the table by his window. Am I tired now? he thought. No, I'm not tired. Disappointed? No, not disappointed either. Embittered? Dejected? No.

He was nothing. And I will stay nothing forever, he thought.

Then he fell asleep while the moon shone big and round into his tiny room.

16

The cricket trudged through the forest. The trees cast sombre looks in his direction and in the distance the thrush was singing a sombre song.

Everything is sombre, he thought, sitting down on a log.

He didn't want to think about anything because all his thoughts hurt, but he started thinking anyway. The sombre feeling is driving my thoughts, he thought. He imagined it standing in his head, among his thoughts, and using a thick branch from the rosebush to hurry them along, hitting them on their backs. But his thoughts couldn't go anywhere and just raced after each other and desperately tried to hold on to each other.

Why? thought the cricket. But every time he thought 'why', the sombre feeling lashed out harder.

I'm not even chirping any more, he thought. He tried

to chirp, but his voice sounded hoarse and sad. Useless chirping, he thought bitterly.

'I'm at my wit's end,' he said to himself finally, and sat there feeling helpless.

The trees around him turned black, and the sky turned black too, and with it, the sun in the middle of the sky. A black wind rose and black letters from one animal to another flew high overhead.

Now and then the cricket looked at himself. His coat had turned black and he had black feet and black wings. Inside his head his thoughts were now as black as ink and slinking past the sombre feeling, which loomed darkly and menacingly over them. If I cried now, he thought, my tears would be black. But he didn't cry.

He sat there all that day. The sun set, but the cricket didn't notice because everything was already black.

The moon appeared, black and round in the black distance.

The cricket lay down on the ground. He couldn't take another step. But it wasn't until the middle of the night that he fell asleep.

'Ah! He's asleep,' he heard. 'Our turn!'

They were black dreams, hurtling towards him and swerving in and out of each other's path to crumple his head and pound on it. All the time roaring with laughter.

When the sun rose, the cricket woke up. Where am I? he thought. He looked around. Nowhere, he decided.

He couldn't move very well. Every last bit of him stung and ached.

What should I do? he thought. He didn't know. But he stood up and walked on. I have to keep going, he thought.

Faraway, at the top of a tree, the thrush started singing again and the wind blew a small letter to the cricket:

Hello Cricket,
    This is just a short letter for no reason.
    Bye,

                    SQUIRREL

The cricket read the letter and sighed deeply. Then he picked up his pace. Maybe that's all I need to do, he thought. Just force myself to pick up my pace. 'Hello, Squirrel,' he said. 'This is a sombre person walking here for no reason. Bye.'

17

The elephant decided to move to the top of the oak.

Once I'm living there, he thought, I'll be sure not to fall down. Just like the squirrel.

He found it a wise decision. Or at least well considered.

He lifted his bed onto his back, climbed the oak, put his bed on the highest branch, lost his balance, and fell.

Dazed, he lay on the ground for a while. But he got up again, hoisted his table onto his back, climbed up, put the table down and lost his balance once more.

He worked like that all day. Big lumps appeared all over his body, but he kept at it. His chair, his cupboard, his floor, his walls, his roof, his woolly hat: he carried it all up.

By early evening his house was ready and he was standing in front of the door, which he had carried up last. Now I can live safely, he thought, and went in. He sat down at the table and looked around contentedly.

Still, there was one thing missing. The elephant scratched behind his ear and pondered. He didn't know what it was. But it was still missing, he was sure of that. A lamp! Suddenly he'd worked it out.

The elephant didn't own a lamp.

It was already twilight when he stood in front of the beech and called up, 'Squirrel!'

The squirrel came out and looked down.

'Hello, Elephant,' he said.

'I've moved,' the elephant said.

'Oh,' said the squirrel.

'I live in the oak now,' the elephant said. 'We're neighbours.'

The squirrel nodded. It was quiet for a moment. Then the elephant cleared his throat.

'I just don't have a lamp,' he said.

The squirrel didn't say anything.

'I wanted to ask…' the elephant said. 'May I borrow your lamp for tonight? I mean, I'm not sure yet where things are, and without a lamp I might bump into them. Or even get lost. In my own house! It could happen. Next thing I'll step through the front door and fall out of the tree. Imagine! That would be terrible.'

The squirrel didn't say anything, just went inside, took

his lamp down from the ceiling, climbed down and gave it to the elephant.

'Thanks,' said the elephant. 'Will you come to visit soon?'

'All right,' said the squirrel.

The elephant walked over to the oak and climbed it. He hung the lamp from the ceiling. Then he could see exactly where everything was: his table, his bed, his chair, his cupboard. He sat down at the table and looked around contentedly. What a lovely home, he thought.

He stood up again and, without actually deciding on it, climbed onto the table and grabbed the lamp. Don't do it, he thought. Just for a sec, he thought. No, don't! Just for a fraction of a second. No!! Yes!!

He swung out and back on the lamp.

'Squirrel!' he called, though he knew the squirrel wasn't there.

Maybe he swung too hard or too high, or maybe the lamp hadn't been hung properly, but suddenly he was flying through the air, lamp and all. And because the lamp was attached to the ceiling, and the ceiling to the walls, and the walls to the floor, everything flew through the air behind him and landed with a tremendous racket on the ground under the oak.

Oh no... thought the elephant as he raised his eyes and saw his broken bed, his fork and two table legs next to him in the grass.

But at least I've lived in the oak, he thought. Now I can always say that I lived in the oak for a while... yeah, it was nice... great view... but, well...

18

The bear was sitting in front of his house, thinking about honey cake and the smell of sweet willow pie and the distinct taste of thistle tart, when the cricket passed by, deep in thought.

'You don't happen to have any cake or pie or tart with you?' asked the bear.

The cricket looked up and said, 'No.'

'Oh,' said the bear. 'Come and visit anyway.'

The cricket went inside.

The bear said he didn't have anything in the house, and poured two frugal cups of the black tea he only drank reluctantly. 'Can't be helped,' he said.

The cricket told him he was sombre and had a sombre feeling in his head.

'What's it look like?' the bear asked.

'I don't know,' the cricket said. 'Grey, I think.'

'What's it taste like?' the bear asked.

'Bitter,' said the cricket. Sometimes he felt like he could taste the sombre feeling.

The bear nodded. 'I know what you mean,' he said. 'I once encountered a sombre pie.'

It was at a birthday party far from the forest. He'd seen some unusual animals there: the emu, the hide beetle, the mara, and a few other animals that rarely showed themselves. He'd forgotten whose birthday it was.

'What did the pie look like?' the cricket asked.

'Also grey,' said the bear. 'Insipid grey. That's what it's called. With grey cream and grey sugar.'

The cricket sighed.

'It was in the middle of the table,' the bear said. 'Nobody dared eat it.'

He looked at the cricket. But the cricket was staring into his empty cup.

'But I did,' the bear said at last. 'There's not a pie in the world I wouldn't dare eat, Cricket.'

He jumped up and looked at the cricket with blazing eyes.

'Pie, cake or tart, I'm not scared of any of them!' he shouted.

'What did it taste like?' the cricket asked.

'Awful,' the bear said, sitting down again. 'Bitter and awful. But I ate it. Down to the last crumb.'

The cricket nodded, while the sombre feeling in his head kicked hard against the back of his skull.

'Everyone stood around in a circle, deeply impressed,' the bear said.

He explained that afterwards it was a really fun birthday. He danced with the monitor lizard and there were lots of cakes too: mild cakes, friendly cakes, cheerful cakes… Everyone thanked him warmly. Because without him, that pie would have still been there on the table and the party would have been a failure.

After the bear had finished his story, it was quiet for a long time. The sun was shining in through the open door and the swallow flew past. The bear poured some more frugal tea into the cricket's cup and the cricket didn't know what to say.

'I once ate an inconsolable cake too…' the bear said. But the cricket felt that it was time to go.

He said goodbye to the bear and walked off through the forest. The sombre feeling swung restlessly from one side of his head to the other and a big black cloud had covered the sun.

19

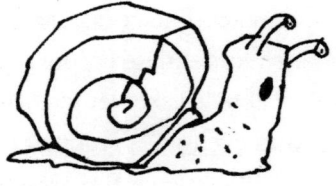

The snail was lying in the sunlight under the plane tree, thinking about things, when the cricket walked past.

'Hello, Snail,' said the cricket.

The snail looked up, stuck his tentacles forward a little and said, 'Hello, Cricket.'

The cricket stopped and said, 'I'm sombre, Snail.'

The snail frowned, raised his head slightly, tilted it, stared at the cricket for a long time and said, 'I'm a lot sombre-er.'

'How awful,' said the cricket.

'How awful?' said the snail, and an expression of surprise appeared on his face. 'How heavy, you mean.'

'How heavy,' said the cricket.

'Yes, very heavy,' said the snail, who launched into an elaborate story about how heavy it was to be so sombre, but he wasn't one to give up and whistle a tune or start dancing instead. The cricket shouldn't think that. Heaviness was not something he, the snail, avoided.

The cricket let his head slump between his shoulders and eventually stopped listening.

'Do you suffer from it?' he asked, when the snail stopped talking for a moment to wipe some slime off his mouth.

'What?' said the snail, looking bewildered. I've never seen him look bewildered before, thought the cricket.

'Do you suffer from it?' he asked again.

The snail didn't know what suffering was, but he answered, 'Yes.' And then, to be on the safe side, he added, 'But in a way, not really, no.'

'Oh,' said the cricket.

The snail then continued his story and summed up the enormous weight of his sombreness and all its protuberances – that was how he described it.

Maybe I'm only slightly sombre, thought the cricket. Maybe my sombreness hardly even counts. But the sombre feeling was still in his head and it didn't want to go away.

'I'm terribly sombre,' he said, when the snail stopped to catch his breath for a moment.

'Ah,' said the snail. 'Terribly sombre, is it? I see. I'm sure it doesn't take much for you to be terribly sombre,

Cricket. But you're mistaken. Your sombreness is nothing compared to mine.' An unfamiliar sparkle had appeared in the snail's eye.

'You'll never be as sombre as me,' he went on. And slowly, and in detail, he listed all the things he could think of about himself that nobody else compared to. His breast swelled so much that he hardly fitted into his shell any more. One of the sides started creaking, and on his head his tentacles were swinging from side to side as if he was waving benignly to a crowd of insignificant spectators.

'Oh,' the cricket repeated every now and then.

Towards midday the snail's voice grew husky and he couldn't say any more.

'I'll be off,' the cricket said.

The snail nodded and watched him go. I'm always more everything, he thought. But most of all, I'm slow. He was disappointed that the cricket hadn't mentioned how slow he was, because if he had, he could have told him a *real* story… He'd still only be at the very start of it. He sighed, turned his head, and looked anxiously at the crack in his shell.

20

I'm lost, the cricket thought, battered and lost.

He was sitting on a stump in the middle of the forest. The sombre feeling kept bumping into the back of his forehead, as if it was wandering round in the dark and didn't know the way.

If you're sombre, thought the cricket, you're lots more besides. Desperate, mournful, distressed, sorrowful, lonely. Sombre brings all that in its wake.

'Sombre!' he shouted suddenly, without knowing why. His voice sounded hollow and miserable.

The crow heard him and landed next to him. 'Did you call me?' she asked.

'No,' said the cricket.

'Oh,' said the crow.

'I'm sombre, Crow,' the cricket said. 'I'm really sombre.'

The crow looked at him and scratched the back of her head. She frowned and walked around the cricket, then lay down on her back and looked under the cricket's wings and at his throat.

'No,' she said, 'you're not sombre at all.'

'Not sombre?' the cricket said. 'I'm really, really sombre.'

'Far from it,' the crow replied.

'Far from it?' the cricket said. 'I'm horribly sombre!'

But the crow shook her head. 'You're not in the least, tiny little bit sombre,' she said.

'Yes, I am!' the cricket cried.

'Not!'

'I am!'

'No.'

They faced off menacingly, both stamping their feet on the ground.

'Ask the ant!' cried the cricket.

'The ant?' the crow croaked. 'The ant? Ask me! I know what it is!'

'You don't have a clue what it is!' the cricket shrieked.

'I know!' the crow bellowed.

'And this feeling in my head? What's that?'

'Air.'

'Air?' the cricket shouted. 'Are you saying it's air?'

'Heavy air,' the crow cawed. 'Maybe even black air. But air.'

The cricket didn't say anything else. His legs gave way beneath him and his head sank to the ground as he started sobbing. Tears streamed out onto the dark earth between the grass. 'Tears of air,' he whispered.

'Yes,' cawed the crow. 'They're tears of air. Now you're finally talking sense.' She flew over to the lowest branch of the beech.

'Sombre…' she croaked mockingly. 'I never…!'

After the crow had disappeared between the trees, cawing angrily, it took the cricket a long time to calm his desperate sobbing.

So I'm not sombre, the cricket thought. Now I'm completely baffled.

He tried to lift his wings to the heavens, but they were too heavy for him. He rolled over and stayed there, lying on his back.

I'm very cheerful, he thought. I chirp, I dance, just look at me…

But nobody saw him lying there in the sunlight in a small pool of tears.

21

The elephant wrote a letter to the oak.

Dear Oak,

  There is something I would like to ask you.

  I would very much like to climb you just once without falling.

  If you approve, I will tell everyone that you are the best, the strongest and the most beautiful tree that exists, whatever you like, and that nobody else can swish and rustle the way you swish and rustle.

  I am prepared tell everyone all about you, whatever you think the others should know.

  You can decide for yourself how I get back down, as long as you make sure it's not by falling.

  And I will also ask the squirrel if you can swing on his lamp sometime.

That is the most delightful thing ever, Oak.
It's actually the direct opposite of falling.

ELEPHANT

After sending the letter, the elephant sat down under the oak to wait for an answer.

But no answer came.

Now and then he looked up. It's bound to be a no, he thought.

Once he was sure that an answer wasn't going to come, he stood up, folded his ears back against his head, sighed and started to climb.

I'll just have to fall, then, he thought.

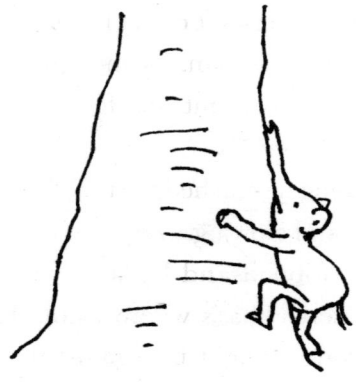

22

The cricket was walking through the forest. But he didn't know where he was going. The sombre feeling in his head was blocking all of his plans and thoughts.

He walked out of the forest, shuffled through the meadow, dragged himself across the steppe and came to the desert.

It was hot, but the cricket didn't feel it.

I don't know where I am, he thought. He kept his eyes on the ground and put one foot in front of the other.

Towards evening he reached the middle of the desert. The sun set, big and glowing.

The cricket stopped and looked around. Oh, he thought, the desert. That's where I am. The sombre feeling was kicking straight up against the top of his skull. It must be standing on its head, thought the cricket.

Suddenly he saw an enormous black something in front of him.

The cricket backed up a step and waited. Things went quiet inside his head.

He brushed a feeler over his dry lips. I know what that is, he thought. He didn't know how he knew, but he knew that he knew.

He stumbled, lowered himself slowly onto one side, rolled over and lay there on his back. Sand trickled into his eyes and ears.

The black monster came closer and bent over him.

'I can't,' the cricket whispered. 'I can't go on.'

Then he felt a giant hand lift him up.

He couldn't move at all.

He felt the dark breath of Sombreness – because that was what the enormous thing was, Sombreness – brushing over his face. A great chill spread through his body. Now I'm going to disappear, he thought. Now...

Then he fell, spinning round and round, and that was the last thing he knew.

The next morning he woke up in the sand in the middle of the desert. The sun was shining on him.

The cricket opened his eyes. The enormous sombreness was gone. The desert was flat and empty and quivering in the sun.

But the sombre feeling in his head was still there.

And I'm still here too, thought the cricket.

He stood up. I'll go back, he thought, and he set off for the forest. He wasn't shuffling any more, but striding with long steps, and now and then he even broke into a jog. The sombre feeling splashed around in his head, as if there was room to spare in there.

Beads of sweat ran down his face and his feelers were glowing.

He thought about the enormous sombreness. What did it want? he thought. To take me with it? But where? Did it let me go? Was that why I fell? Was it by accident?

He didn't know. And what was the enormous sombreness doing in the middle of the desert anyway? he thought. Waiting for me? No, that can't be right. It was after something else, it must have been.

But the cricket had no idea what that something else could be, what Sombreness wanted.

23

When the cricket got home, he realised that the next day was his birthday.

He rubbed his face, shook his head and wrote a letter to all the animals:

My birthday's off.
 Sorry.
> CRICKET

He baked a small, sad cake in case someone didn't read the letter, and put his table outside in front of the bramble.

On the morning of his birthday, he mumbled to himself, 'Happy nothing at all, Cricket.'

'No, it isn't,' he mumbled back.

He put the sad cake down and sat at the head of the table.

The sun was shining, it was a hot day and, high in the sky, the swallow flew past every now and then.

Nobody came. The cricket sat there all day, looking out over his deserted table. It's my birthday, he thought now and then. The sombre feeling filled his entire head and all his thoughts hurt. Can thoughts bleed? he wondered. If thoughts can bleed, they're bleeding now.

At the end of the afternoon, the squirrel walked past the bramble bush and saw the cricket sitting there. Hesitantly, he approached.

'I thought I'd drop by anyway,' he said. He coughed.

The cricket nodded.

'I brought something too,' the squirrel said. 'Here.' He gave the cricket a present.

It was a woolly hat you could pull down over your head.

'Shall I put it on?' the cricket asked.

'If you like.'

The cricket put the hat on and pulled it down over his head.

The squirrel put a grey grain of cake in his mouth and decided not to take any more.

'Are you still sombre?' he asked, after they had sat silently across from each other for a long time.

'Yes,' the cricket said from under the hat.

The sun was already starting to go down behind the trees.

'We're not going to laugh,' the cricket said.

'No,' said the squirrel.

'Or sing.'

'No.'

'And we're definitely not going to dance.'

'No.'

'In fact, you're not really here, Squirrel,' the cricket said.

'No, I'm not really here,' said the squirrel. 'Nobody's here.'

'No,' the cricket said. 'That's it. Nobody is here, really.'

With the light already fading, the squirrel stood up. 'So,' he said. 'I'll be off.'

'Yes,' said the cricket.

He didn't say anything else, and the squirrel said goodbye and left.

The cricket sat at his table with his hat over his eyes. The moon rose over the forest and shone on the bramble and the cricket's hat.

Later I'll write you a letter, the cricket thought. One saying, Thank you, Squirrel. But not now.

THE CRICKET'S HEALING

He stood up, took off the hat, threw the cake into the bushes, carried the table inside and lay down on his bed.

He looked up at his ceiling. 'Later', he thought, does that actually even exist?

He didn't know.

24

Sitting at his table, the cricket thought, I have to do something. But what?

The sombre feeling in his head was as heavy and unbudgeable as ever, and now and then it gave him a hard thump.

'What do you want?' the cricket asked.

It remained quiet in his head. To never answer, the cricket thought bitterly, that's what you want.

At his wit's end, he decided to write a letter.

Dear Sombre Feeling,
 How are you?
 I'm sure you know how I am.
 Is there something I can do for you, perhaps?
 Shall I answer questions for you?
 Maybe you don't know the answers to questions I do know the answers to.

(Just as you know questions for answers I don't know the questions for.)

If I do that for you, will you go away?
Shall I think of somewhere beautiful you can go?
Like the ocean? Or the moon?
I would be very glad to help you if you leave.
You're not staying forever, are you?

THE OWNER OF THE HEAD YOU'RE IN

The wind rose, the window blew open and the letter flew up, swirled around and disappeared.

Then the wind died down again.

It was very quiet in the cricket's head.

The sombre feeling is reading the letter now, the cricket thought. But he didn't know that for sure and he wondered if he was possibly making it all up, even the sombre feeling.

But a little later the wind rose again and a letter fell on the table.

It was a dark letter with thick black writing, saying:

GRISHRGRHT

That was all. There wasn't a sender underneath either.

The cricket lowered his head. 'Thank you very much, Sombre Feeling,' he said and punched himself in the head.

He fell over, chair and all, and the table fell on top of him.

The letter was lying exactly over his face.

'Grishrgrht,' he read again.

So there's nothing I can do for it, the cricket thought. It knows the answers to all questions, of course.

The sombre feeling seemed to stand up. It started drilling. But what was it drilling into?

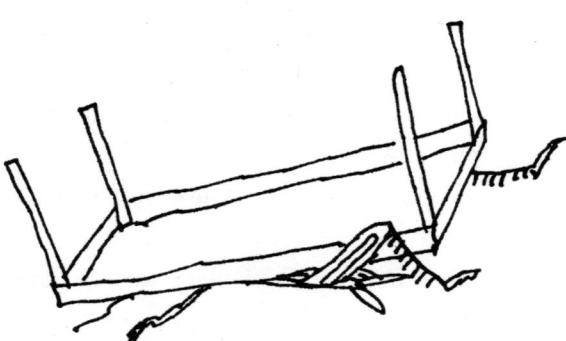

25

The elephant was ill. Lying on his back on the moss under the oak, he looked up at its top branches with burning eyes.

The squirrel was sitting next to him.

Now and then the elephant groaned for a moment, or shivered.

'Maybe I'll never climb another tree,' he said suddenly.

The squirrel nodded. Then it was quiet again.

'What would happen if *you* never climbed another tree?' the elephant asked a little later.

'I don't know,' the squirrel said. The sun was shining and he thought about the glittering ripples on the river. What would happen if I never saw that again? he thought.

'What are these things?' the elephant asked, pointing with the tip of his trunk at two big drops slowly rolling down his glowing cheeks.

The squirrel studied the drops and said, 'They're tears.'

'Oh,' the elephant said and let them fall on his side. He pondered for a long time, then said, with his back to the squirrel, 'Maybe I'll never swing on your lamp any more either.'

The squirrel poked at the moss with one toe. That would be really terrible, he thought. But he didn't say it.

It was a hot day, and the squirrel leant back and closed his eyes.

Suddenly he woke with a start. The elephant had disappeared.

The squirrel looked around.

Then he realised where to look. The elephant was standing on the lowest branch of the oak. 'I've lost the knack,' he said, swaying and with his teeth chattering.

'I thought you were never going to climb another tree,' the squirrel said.

'Yes,' the elephant said, 'I thought so too. But what if something terrible happened because I wasn't climbing? Something I've never even heard of?'

The squirrel didn't reply.

'What then?' the elephant asked. His cheeks were glowing and he looked at the squirrel with big eyes.

The squirrel didn't know how to answer and the elephant put a foot on the next branch. But he really had lost the knack. He fell backwards on the ground with a dull thud.

There was a kink in his trunk and he said softly, 'Ow, ow.'

The squirrel laid a blanket over him and said, 'Try to get some sleep.'

'Now I'll really never climb again, Squirrel,' the elephant said, hitting his head with his front legs. 'No matter what!' he shouted in a hoarse voice. Not to the squirrel, but to himself. 'Fine,' he mumbled, 'I believe you. But what if…' He tried to wave his trunk but couldn't. 'No more ifs,' he said. 'No more ifs ever again.'

Then he fell silent.

But after a while he turned to the squirrel and asked, 'Do you think that my condition is fatal?'

The squirrel didn't know what fatal was and said, 'Shh. Sleep.'

Then the elephant fell asleep and in his sleep he got better.

26

Under the ground the mole and the earthworm were sitting together in the dark.

'Have you heard the news, Earthworm?' the mole asked.

'What news?' asked the earthworm.

'The cricket's sombre,' said the mole.

'Really?'

'Yes. He's become it.'

'Oh…'

They both looked at the ground.

'Shouldn't we congratulate him?' the earthworm asked.

'Yes,' said the mole. 'We should.'

They wrote a letter to the cricket:

THE CRICKET'S HEALING

Dear Cricket,
  Sincere congratulations on having become sombre.
  We still haven't managed it yet.

MOLE AND EARTHWORM

They had been trying to become sombre for a very long time, but they never succeeded. They stood in front of black mirrors, let their shoulders droop, frowned, thought about the sun, and cast joyless looks in every direction.

'Almost,' they said to each other. 'We're almost there.' But they never made it all the way.

That night they drank black tea and wondered how the cricket had become sombre and what he would do now. 'Will he be really miserable now?' the mole asked.

'I don't know,' the earthworm said, and pushed his nose into the ground.

They stayed there all night. Now and then they talked briefly about melancholy lamentations or regret and calamity. But mostly they just sat in silence.

In the end they started dancing in a corner of the room.

They held each other close as they danced.

'We dance so fabulously,' they said stoically. Because they knew that if they'd been able to dance sombrely, it would have been even more fabulous.

It wasn't until morning that a letter from the cricket arrived in reply.

Dear Mole and Earthworm,
I didn't manage it. It just happened.
I wish I was you.

CRICKET

But the mole and the earthworm didn't read the letter. They were asleep.

27

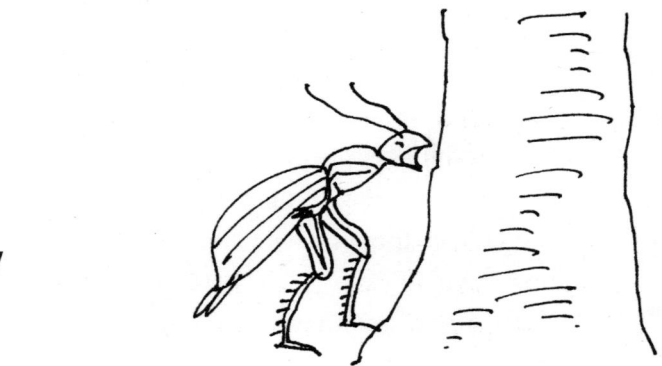

The cricket leant against the linden and let his head hang. The sombre feeling slid forward and pressed heavily on the back of his eyes. Don't, he thought. But he didn't say anything.

He heard knocking.

'Yes,' he said, looking around, but he couldn't see anyone. Whoever it was knocked again. The sound was coming from the linden.

'Yes,' said the cricket, now facing the tree.

It was quiet for a moment.

'What?' called a voice inside the linden.

'Was that knock for me?' the cricket asked.

'Who's me?' the voice asked. It was the woodworm, who was at work inside the trunk.

'The cricket,' the cricket said.

'The what?' shouted the woodworm.

'The cricket!' the cricket shouted.

Another moment of quiet.

'What are you doing?' the woodworm asked.

The cricket thought for a moment and said, 'I'm sombre.'

'You're what?' the woodworm asked.

'Sombre,' the cricket said.

'What?'

'Sombre!'

'I can't hear you properly. What are you?'

'Sombre!' the cricket bellowed as loud as he could, with his mouth to the trunk of the linden.

The woodworm knocked on the wood a few times.

'I still can't make you out,' she said. 'Why don't you come in?'

'How?' the cricket asked.

'What's that?'

'How?!' the cricket yelled.

'Goodness,' the woodworm said. 'I'm sure you think you're being perfectly clear. How-how… what's that supposed to mean?'

The cricket didn't reply.

'Are you going somewhere?' the woodworm asked.

'No.'

'Why not?'

The cricket didn't know.

'Is it because you don't have anywhere to go?' the woodworm asked. The cricket nodded but didn't answer.

'Do you know what I think?' the woodworm asked.

'No,' said the cricket.

'I think you're a weirdo,' the woodworm said.

'Oh,' said the cricket.

'Do you agree or not?'

The cricket held his tongue.

The woodworm stuck her head out. 'You and Air,' she said. 'A couple of weirdos.'

She pulled her head back in and said, 'I don't have any time for weirdos.'

'What do you have time for?' the cricket asked.

'What?' said the woodworm.

The cricket stayed quiet. What do I have time for myself? he thought, and shrugged. Nothing, he decided. It was as if the sombre feeling had swallowed all his time.

'Goodbye, Weirdo,' the woodworm said and disappeared into a thick side bough of the linden.

'Goodbye, Woodworm,' said the cricket.

A weirdo, the cricket thought. So I'm a weirdo. Me, who once chirped and sang…

He tried to sigh, or cry, if necessary, but nothing happened. He just sat there.

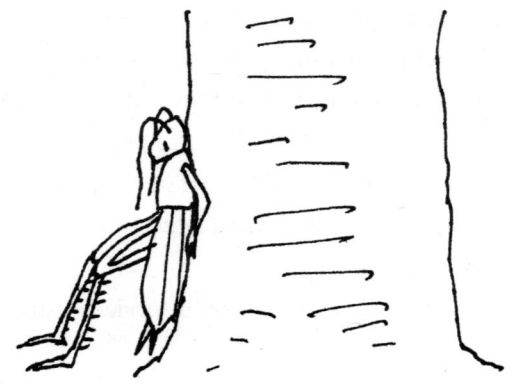

28

One morning the elephant fell asleep under the oak.

It was quiet in the forest. The bumblebee was buzzing in the rosebush and the smell of honeysuckle was spiralling up between the trees.

Almost immediately after drifting off, the elephant stood up, stuck his front legs straight out towards the oak and began climbing.

I seem to be asleep, he thought, making sure to keep his eyes shut.

Calmly and with a straight back, he climbed the tree. What a wonderful nap, he thought.

He heard a bustling overhead. The hustle and bustle of a party, he thought. What fun! A party in my sleep!

By the time he reached the top of the oak, he was feeling hot. I think I'm in the desert, he thought. The bustling grew louder and the wind blew the top of the oak from side to side.

Someone's tugging on me, thought the elephant. Someone must want to dance with me. How nice!

'Okay,' he said and started dancing. He didn't know who he was dancing with because he still had his eyes shut. I'm asleep, after all, he thought.

'How wonderfully we're dancing,' he said. His partner only rustled and didn't answer.

'Shall I do a pirouette?' the elephant asked. 'Would you mind? A teensy little pirouette?'

Then he heard a voice, 'Elephant! Elephant!'

He opened his eyes and looked down. Far below him he saw the squirrel, standing at the foot of the tree. The elephant had just raised one foot and was about to begin his pirouette.

'Yes?' he called and lost his balance. He fell down through the oak's branches, dragging leaves and twigs with him, and landed on the ground at the squirrel's feet with an enormous crash.

'Why do I always wake up?' he groaned when he finally opened his eyes. 'I always wake up.' Tears were welling up in his eyes.

The squirrel sat next to him.

'I'm sorry, Elephant,' he said. 'I wanted to ask if you'd like to come and visit.'

The elephant wiped the tears from his cheeks with his trunk.

'Have you still got that lamp?' he whispered.

'Yes,' the squirrel said.

Soon after, they set out for the beech. The elephant was leaning on the squirrel, who carried him up the tree to make sure he got there safely.

'I mean, your ceiling lamp?' the elephant asked, halfway up.

'Yes,' the squirrel panted. The elephant was heavy and the squirrel's house was at the very top of the beech.

29

When the salamander heard that the cricket was sombre, she decided to open a shop.

If somebody's sombre, she thought, it's bound to catch on. Mark my words. If somebody has cake, everybody else will want some too.

She opened her sombreness shop under the acacia.

Early in the morning the swan came by. 'What kind of sombreness do you have in stock?' he asked.

The salamander looked at him. A distinguished customer, she thought. 'A variety of sombrenesses,' she said. 'I have no doubt you'll find one to your liking in my inventory.'

She took a number of different kinds from the shelves and arranged them on the counter.

'This is an elegant sombreness,' she said. 'And this sombriety is unusually restrained.'

'Ah,' said the swan, holding a small, black yet translucent sombriety up to his face, 'how lovely.'

'Shall all who see me bemoan me?' he asked.

'They certainly will,' the salamander said. 'And all the more grievously if you discreetly wipe away the occasional tear.'

The swan also looked at a bleak wintry sombreness, a musty morbid one, an acrid spiteful one and a heart-rending sallow one. But he settled on the unusually restrained sombriety and left with a serious expression on his face.

Later that afternoon, the cricket was passing the salamander's shop and stopped in front of the window.

The salamander saw him and came out. She clapped her hand over her mouth. 'Oh…' she said. 'What a magnificent sombreness…' She shook her head and studied the cricket from all sides.

'If you ever want to part with it, Cricket…' she said thoughtfully. 'I think it's dazzling. Dazzling!'

But the cricket looked past her at the darkness between the trees. Inside his head, his sombre feeling was racing from one ear to the other with a frightful pounding.

'I don't know,' he said.

'If you ever change your mind…' the salamander said.

New customers appeared. They were looking for small sombre moods for a single evening, but also years of sombreness, or sombre feelings with prickles or slippery scales.

The salamander was very cheerful and leapt around behind her counter. She didn't disappoint anyone.

At the end of the afternoon she covered the leftover sombrenesses with a black cloth. Otherwise they'll get bleached, she thought, and nobody will want them any more.

The cricket had already walked deep into the forest without knowing where he was going. A low sun was shining through the trees. It was a hot day, but the cricket was cold and shivery.

30

The cricket was walking up and down in front of his house with his head down. His wings were heavy and drooping and his feet were slow and swollen.

Why am I sombre? he thought. Why?

He'd asked himself that question a hundred times without coming up with an answer, but he still kept on asking it. Why? Why?

I'm always so cheerful otherwise, he thought. He pictured himself flying and jumping through the forest and he heard himself chirping. Is that me? he thought. And is this me now?

He shook his head.

Maybe the sombre feeling has made a mistake, he thought, suddenly stopping his pacing. Maybe it thinks I'm someone else!

He tapped his head. 'Sombre Feeling,' he said.

It stayed quiet.

He'd expected that, and continued. 'Do you actually know where you are?' he asked. 'Do you think perhaps you're in the beetle's head? Or the crow's? Then you're wrong. You are located inside the cricket's head. That's me. The cricket. You didn't know that, did you? I'm always cheerful. *Always,* Sombre Feeling!'

Again he stopped talking and listened carefully. But he couldn't hear anything and he couldn't feel any thumping or grating inside his head. 'A mistake is nothing to be ashamed of, Sombre Feeling,' he said. 'I get things wrong all the time. Sometimes I start chirping when I actually meant to fly. And sometimes... But don't get me started...'

He held his breath for a moment, looked around and then continued. 'I'm not blaming you for anything, Sombre Feeling. Really, I'm not. You can leave my head with your head held high.'

He cleared his throat. He found that last sentence a bit peculiar. But beautiful too. He loved it when heads were held high. If only my own head was held high, he thought.

Nothing happened. 'Just go,' the cricket said. 'Go on. I'm the cricket. *The cricket*, Sombre Feeling. The cricket! Not the beetle or the crow or the squid or the termite. The cricket. You've made a mistake! You're lost! Quick, go!'

It was early in the morning, the sun was shining through the linden branches, and in the river the carp stuck her cheery head up out of the water.

The cricket didn't know what else to say. There was no reaction inside his head. The sombre feeling was staying just where it was.

Then the cricket tugged on his head, swung it from side to side, banged it on the ground, squeezed his feelers as hard as he could, and fell over.

Stretched out on his back, he lay in the dry dust under the linden. It's not lost, he thought. I'm where it has to be. It's home.

31

The cricket was sitting in the grass. The sombre feeling was bashing the inside of his head with sticks.

The elephant was sitting next to him. 'If you climb,' he said, 'you're never sombre. You can't be.'

'Why not?' the cricket asked.

'It's a law of nature,' the elephant said.

'And when you fall?' the cricket asked.

'When I fall,' the elephant said, 'it hurts. But I'm not sombre.' He scrunched up his forehead and thought deeply. 'No,' he said, 'it doesn't make me sombre.'

The cricket fell silent.

'We could climb together…' the elephant said.

'Are you sure it never makes you sombre?' the cricket asked.

'Yes,' said the elephant. 'Very sure. I, the elephant, have never been sombre while climbing a tree and I have never been sombre falling out of one either.'

A little later they were climbing the oak.

'You lead the way,' the elephant said.

It was a beautiful day.

'Isn't climbing fabulous?' the elephant said every now and then.

The cricket didn't reply. The sombre feeling in his head had got its hands on some kind of squeaky whistle and was blowing it as hard as it could next to his inner ear.

When they made it to the top, the elephant said, 'Made it.'

'What?' the cricket asked.

But the elephant started flapping his ears and trumpeting cheerfully.

The sombre feeling in the cricket's head was holding a particularly shrill note as long as possible. Even though he knew it wouldn't help, the cricket pressed his hands against his ears.

The elephant stopped trumpeting, coughed and said, 'I know I should never stand on one leg. And definitely not on top of the oak. And I know for certain that I should never do a pirouette.'

He stood on one leg and got ready to start a pirouette.

'But, you know…' he said and shrugged.

Then he lost his balance.

'Whoa!' he cried, wrapping his trunk around the cricket's nose to save himself.

They fell together. Thick branches snapped and whipped against them.

When they opened their eyes a little later, the elephant had a big lump on the back of his head. 'But I'm not sombre,' he groaned softly.

The cricket's wings were bruised and he had a broken nose. There were two lumps on his back and he couldn't move his legs. 'I am,' he said. Because the sombre feeling now had a drum and it was drumming as loud and as triumphantly as it could in the middle of the cricket's head.

The elephant looked at him and said in a hoarse voice, 'I don't know what else to say.' Carefully he ran his trunk over the back of his head. 'Ow,' he mumbled, 'ow.'

The cricket tried to get up to flee the drumming in his head, but he couldn't manage it. 'Maybe you can swing on Squirrel's lamp,' the elephant said. 'That never makes me sombre either.' Again the cricket tried to stand up. The drumming had become deafening.

The elephant got up, brushed off the dust and stumbled away.

The cricket just lay there on his back while the sombre feeling, without interrupting its drumming, started blowing a bugle as well, loud, blaring and unrelenting. Maybe there are two of them, he thought.

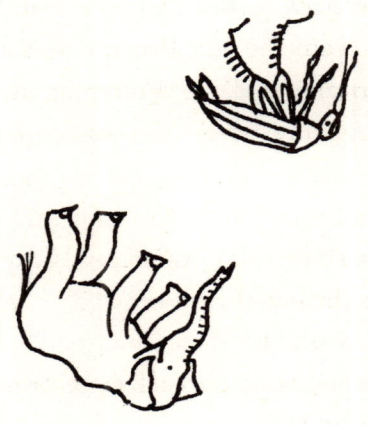

32

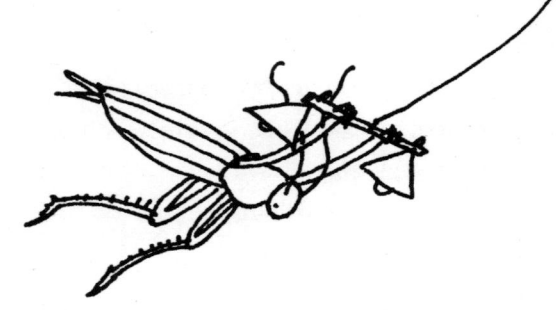

The cricket knocked on the squirrel's door. It was early evening.

'Yes,' the squirrel said.

'It's me,' said the cricket. 'The sombre cricket.'

'Come in,' said the squirrel, opening the door.

The cricket stepped in.

'Cricket, how delightful,' the squirrel said. 'Would you like some tea? Or something else?'

Inside the cricket's head the sombre feeling was blowing a kind of tin horn the cricket had never heard before. The sound was loud and ugly.

'I'm not delightful,' the cricket said. 'I'm sombre.'

'Have a seat,' said the squirrel.

'I wanted to ask,' the cricket said, 'if I could swing on your lamp.'

'Of course,' said the squirrel.

'Maybe it will stop me being sombre.'

'Maybe,' the squirrel said.

They drank their tea.

'Do you hear that?' the cricket asked. In his head the sombre feeling was singing like a choir rehearsing a really miserable song. The squirrel pressed his ear against the side of the cricket's head, but he couldn't hear anything.

When they'd finished their tea, the cricket said, 'Shall I start swinging now?'

'If you like,' the squirrel said.

The cricket climbed onto the table, grabbed the lamp and began swinging. The squirrel sat down on the side of his bed.

The cricket swung in silence for a while, the sombre feeling in his head swinging silently with him.

'When you're over the table, you have to call out, "Hello, Squirrel!"' said the squirrel.

Every time he came over the table, the cricket said, 'Hello, Squirrel.'

'You have to swing higher,' the squirrel said.

The cricket swung higher.

'Higher still,' said the squirrel, while letting out an almost imperceptible sigh.

Then the cricket fell, lamp and all, on the table. The table broke and all the bits of the cricket that weren't already hurting now hurt as well.

But the sombre feeling in his head seemed to be cheering or crushing something into dust – the cricket couldn't tell exactly what it was doing.

'I'm sorry,' he mumbled. 'I'm sorry, Squirrel.'

'Are you still sombre?' the squirrel asked.

The cricket nodded.

They drank another cup of tea surrounded by the pieces of the table and the lamp.

'I'm sorry,' the cricket said after each mouthful.

'It doesn't matter,' the squirrel replied each time, and when the cricket's cup was empty, he filled it again.

In the middle of the night, the cricket crept home. The sombre feeling in his head had gone quiet. But it was still there. It's gathering new strength, the cricket thought. He shuddered to think what the sombre feeling might be able to do with new strength.

33

One afternoon the cricket got a letter.

Dear Cricket,

My birthday is coming up soon.
I have heard so much about you.
Almost everyone shakes their head about you.
But not me.
Would you be so kind as to come and sombre up my birthday?
That's what I call it.
I have had more than enough of happy birthdays...
As a gift you could give me a mirror in which I always look gloomy, even when smiling, or if I'm accidentally deeply contented.
I'll make sure there's a dismal cake.
I'm not asking anyone else, because otherwise somebody might have fun!

You are someone I can count on, who definitely won't disappoint me. Or should I say, I hope that you will disappoint me?

MOLE RAT

That same afternoon the cricket wrote back.

Dear Mole Rat,
I can't go on like this.

CRICKET

34

The elephant was lying on the grass under the oak. Every now and then he touched the bump on the back of his head and groaned softly.

Not long before, he had fallen headfirst from the top of the oak. All around him lay leaves and broken twigs and branches.

He could hear a kind of whooshing sound, but couldn't tell if it was inside his head or outside of it. Cautiously, he opened his eyes.

Standing before him was a big, heavy figure with enormous teeth and long dripping hair hanging down in front of its cheeks. It was studying him intently.

'Hello, Elephant,' said the figure.

'Who are you?' the elephant asked.

'Falling,' said the figure. 'I'm Falling.'

'Hello, Falling,' the elephant sighed. He was still too

dazed to be surprised. 'What are you doing here? I've already fallen.'

'I'm waiting for you to climb back up.'

'You'll have to wait a long time,' the elephant said.

'Ah,' said Falling, shrugging his gigantic shoulders, 'how long is long?'

'Long is really long,' the elephant said, touching the back of his head again. 'Long is forever. I know that for a fact!'

Falling pulled out a small book and leafed through it, muttering, 'Forever, forever…' It cleared its throat and said, 'Here it is. "Forever: continually, eternally." Also: "a seemingly endless period of time".'

The elephant squeezed his eyes shut. Now I understand, he thought, and nodded earnestly.

When he reopened his eyes, Falling had disappeared.

The elephant looked around and tried to sit up. Why doesn't anybody else ever fall? he thought. Why always me?

It was quiet. But he still seemed to hear a voice saying, 'Because you fall so beautifully… Nobody falls as beautifully as you…'

Yeah, right, thought the elephant. He hauled himself up and put one foot on the lowest branch of the oak. At the same time, he let out a deep sigh. A *seemingly* endless period of time, he thought. That means sooner or later it does end.

He heard creaking and rustling, but he still couldn't tell if it was inside his head or somewhere far away.

Oh well, he thought, and started climbing.

While climbing, he looked around every now and then. The sun was high in the sky and the ripples on the river were glittering in the distance. Above him the oak leaves were shaking and rustling.

The elephant nodded and started climbing faster.

When he'd almost reached the top, he heard a new voice. 'Hello, Elephant,' said the voice.

The elephant saw a small, elegant figure.

'Who are you?' he asked.

'Climbing,' it answered. 'I'm Climbing. Your climbing.'

As quickly as it had appeared, the figure disappeared again.

My climbing, thought the elephant, so that was *my* climbing... He felt his face glowing with joy.

With one last step, he reached the top of the oak and suddenly he knew who Falling and Climbing were. Climbing is part of me, he thought, and Falling is something to worry about later. And he shouted that last bit loudly in all directions, 'Falling is something to worry about later!'

The squirrel happened to be passing and looked up. He saw the elephant. 'Did you call out something?' he asked.

'Falling is something to worry about later!' the elephant shouted again. He stood on one leg and, with glistening eyes and feeling happier than ever before, tried to do a pirouette.

35

The animals decided to throw a party in the middle of the forest. Against sombreness, they said. For the cricket.

Everyone came and brought a present for the cricket, as if it was his birthday. They gave him cheerful hats, thick winter coats, festive articles that served no useful purpose, and much more.

The cricket was sitting at a big table in the middle. Inside his head, the sombre feeling was sitting on an iron throne and screaming unintelligible orders.

'Thank you, Hippo,' the cricket mumbled. 'Thank you, Butterfly. Thank you, Swan.'

He put the presents down on the ground behind him and leant on the table.

The bear had brought a cake.

'It's a honey cake, Cricket. The tastiest cake I could

think of,' he said. 'Of course, I don't know if you like honey cake too. But I do, at least.'

He put the cake down in front of the cricket. The cricket nodded.

'Or shall I just eat it myself to be on the safe side?' the bear asked. 'That way at least somebody will have eaten something they like.' He picked the cake up again and stuffed it into his mouth.

The animals were very cheerful. As planned. They sang songs about the summer and about the moon and the river's murmuring, and everyone danced with everyone else: the ant with the squirrel, the toad with the elephant, the giraffe with the heron.

It was a warm summer's evening. Stars were twinkling in the sky and the river was gleaming.

Now and then a cheer went up for no reason, just like that.

The glow-worm was glowing on a branch of the willow and the firefly danced with the butterfly under the rosebush.

What a party, they all thought.

Later that night, spirits were even higher. The rhino threw the hippo up in the air, the tortoise forgot herself and raced around in circles, and the snail giggled, stood on his tentacles and tried to walk. The walrus said he had never been as exuberant. 'Because that's what I am, right?' he asked anyone who came close, and everyone said, 'Yes, you're very exuberant, Walrus.' The mole and the earthworm ignored the moonlight and danced in the open air, and the elephant climbed up onto the giraffe's neck, fell to the ground with a thud and cried, 'That doesn't count!'

Animals that didn't know they could laugh burst out laughing, and even the pike and the carp sang and patted each other on the back with their fins.

Only the cricket sat motionless on his chair at the table. Now and then a tear rolled down his cheek. But nobody gave him a second glance.

He drummed slowly on the table and stared at his fingers. Sombre fingers, he thought.

He slid down off the chair and curled up under the table.

Now nobody could see him.

36

The cricket dug a hole behind his house and sat in it. It was a perfect fit. Only the back of his head stuck up above ground.

He put on his black woolly hat and pulled it down over his head.

He stayed there like that all day.

Now and then he heard animals walking past, talking about him.

'This is where the cricket lives.'

'Oh, here?'

'Yes. He's very sombre. I suppose you knew?'

'Yes, I knew that. Everybody knows that.'

'Yes.'

'What would that feel like, do you think?'

'Being sombre?'

'Yes.'

'I can tell you exactly what it's like. You see…' But then their voices died out again.

He heard the wind blowing a letter in under his door and hours later whistling and shrieking as it dragged it away again.

Around noon someone came by and stopped and called, 'Cricket!'

The cricket heard them pacing in front of his house and standing on their toes to look in. A little later he heard them walking on, mumbling, 'He's not there.'

No, thought the cricket. I'm not.

He had hardly any room and could only breathe and think.

It was only when it was completely dark that he climbed out of the hole and went back into the house. He peered for a long time at a jar of sweet buttercups. But he didn't eat anything.

Then he lay down on his bed. What a day… he thought.

In the middle of the night a short letter from the moth, who just wanted to say hello, blew in, and towards morning, the glow-worm whispered through a chink in the wall, 'Can you see me, Cricket?'

The cricket turned his head to the side and saw a small ray of light through the chink in his wall.

'Yes,' he said.

'Very good,' said the glow-worm.

Very good… thought the cricket. What does that mean again? Nothing, he thought. It doesn't mean a thing. Nothing does.

37

When the cricket woke up, the sun was shining and the whole sky was blue.

He tried to get up but the sombre feeling in his head kept pulling him back down. He considered going back to the hole behind his house, but stayed where he was, lying on his back, while thoughts of mud and snowstorms swept over him.

After a while he heard a rustling. The wind was blowing something under his door. It was a small red letter.

For a long time the cricket didn't move. The sombre feeling in his head growled, 'You can't go on like this.'

I can't go on like this, the cricket thought.

'And it's never going to change,' the sombre feeling growled.

And it's never going to change, thought the cricket.

But finally he got up and picked up the letter.

He read:

Dear Cricket,
  I've heard that you're sombre.
  I know what you have to do: you have to get better.
      (WHO I AM IS NOT IMPORTANT)

The cricket read the letter again. Who I am is not important… he thought. Who could that be? He tried to think of animals that weren't important. The mosquito? The moth? The flea? The smelt? The pilot fish?

Nobody is important, he thought. But he didn't know that for sure. Maybe everyone is important in a modest kind of way.

The sombre feeling rumbled in his head.

I'm unimportant anyway, the cricket thought. I am really unimportant. I'm the most unimportant of all.

But he hadn't written this letter.

He read it again. You have to get better… he read. What did that even mean? He didn't know. Get better, get better… he thought. He could vaguely remember knowing what it meant. But he'd forgotten.

The sombre feeling rattled and made grinding sounds in his head.

THE CRICKET'S HEALING

The cricket thought, That feeling *is* important…

He read the letter another couple of times and thought, so I have to get better… It really does say that.

Maybe it's a secret code, he thought. But if that's the case, there might not be anybody who knows what getting better means.

He took a piece of paper and wrote in big letters:

I HAVE TO GET BETTER

Then he stuck the piece of paper to the wall.

If I look at it long enough, maybe I'll find out, he thought. Either way, it's something that has to be done.

To his surprise, he did a little jig. It was only the start of a jig and it was over almost before he knew it. But it was still a jig.

The sombre feeling seemed to be racing furiously to and fro between his forehead and the back of his head.

'Shh,' the cricket said.

He read the words on the page on his wall over and over – until the sun disappeared behind a black cloud and it started to rain.

38

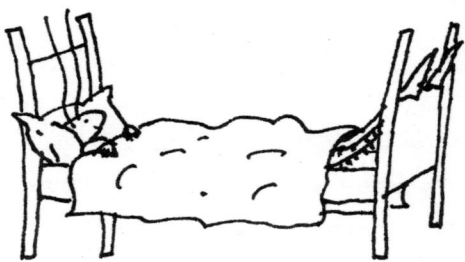

The cricket was in bed. It was the middle of the night. It was stormy and the house was creaking.

The cricket was staring up at the ceiling and he could hear voices coming from all over his room.

'I know how you have to get better,' they called. 'You have to gabble. You have to gargle. You have to shrink. You have to turn pale. You have to swell up. You have to guess. You have to deduce. You have to harbour suspicions…'

'I can't!' the cricket shouted.

'You have to!' the voices shouted back, growing louder and louder.

The window was thrown open and gigantic cakes came flying in.

'Demolish!' they shouted. 'Devour!'

Wings came flying in as well, and fins. The cricket had to put them on and use them to fly and swim away.

'I can't!' he shouted. 'I can't!'

'You have to! You have to!'

Then he heard a thunderous voice inside his head. It was the voice of the sombre feeling. 'Stop,' it said.

The other voices fell silent and his window banged shut again.

Just one little voice was still whining, very quietly: 'You have to be wrong.'

Then silence fell.

The cricket looked at the ceiling and the ceiling looked back and said, 'Yes, Cricket, that's right…'

The sombre feeling curled up inside his head. It's falling asleep, the cricket thought. It can't go on like this either.

Very briefly and very cautiously, so as not to wake it up, the cricket was cheerful.

Then he, too, fell asleep.

39

'Do you ever fall out of a tree?' the elephant asked the squirrel.

They were at the squirrel's house, drinking tea. It was early evening.

'No,' the squirrel said.

'But you climb,' the elephant said. 'How do you do it?'

'I don't know,' the squirrel said, and he really didn't.

The elephant stared seriously at his tea and asked if it was all right if he swung on the lamp for a moment. It was.

Late that night he stepped out of what was left of the squirrel's house and fell with an enormous racket from the top of the beech to the ground.

The next day he had a plan. He disguised himself as the squirrel and went to the oak.

'Hello, Squirrel,' the beetle said when their paths crossed.

'Hello, Beetle,' said the elephant. The beetle stopped for a moment to wonder if the squirrel had always had a trunk, but the elephant walked on, thinking, So I really am the squirrel…

He whistled a tune he thought the squirrel would whistle and put one foot on the oak's lowest branch.

All right, he thought, and said, 'It's me, Oak, the squirrel… I'm just coming up…'

The oak rustled and swung its branches from side to side.

The elephant climbed to the top and then looked out over the whole forest. He could see the desert, the ocean and, in the distance, the mountains.

'I am the squirrel!' he shouted. 'The squirrel!'

Then he fell, plunging straight through the branches and shouting, 'Hey! I'm the squirrel! I never fall!'

He hit the ground with a heavy thud and lay there in a daze.

The squirrel had seen him fall and came running.

When the elephant opened his eyes, he saw the squirrel standing in front of him. 'I shouted,' he groaned.

'What did you shout?' the squirrel asked.

'"I am the squirrel,"' the elephant whispered.

The squirrel didn't say anything.

'What should I have shouted?' the elephant asked with tears in his eyes.

The squirrel helped him up, gently rubbed a few lumps, straightened out his trunk and made sure the elephant looked like the elephant again.

'You can't fool Falling,' the elephant said a little later, when they were walking one step at a time through the forest.

'Do you know what Falling is?' the elephant asked, stopping for a moment.

'No,' the squirrel said.

'Implacable,' the elephant said.

Silently they continued on their way.

40

The sparrow was giving lessons in a corner of the forest.

It was busy and he was running from one student to the next.

He was teaching the elephant to never fall again and had just told him to climb a small tree.

Every time the elephant fell out of the tree, he cried, 'I'll never learn!'

'Don't despair, Elephant,' the sparrow chirped cheerfully. 'You've almost got it.'

The cricket was learning how to get better.

On a big board the sparrow had written:

GETTING BETTER IS BEING BETTER

The cricket copied out the words.

'Very good,' said the sparrow. 'You're halfway there.'

The sombre feeling growled inside the cricket's head.

'Now you have to say "I am better" one hundred times,' the sparrow said.

The cricket started. But after the fifth time, he lost count.

'Doesn't matter,' said the sparrow. 'Start again.'

The cricket started again.

'What a life!' chirped the sparrow as he flew over to the elephant, who was just falling and drilled headfirst into the ground.

By sunset, the elephant could no longer stand. He had dozens of lumps and bumps all over his body.

'You're almost there, Elephant,' the sparrow chirped. 'And you too, Cricket. You're almost better.'

The elephant groaned and the sparrow said he'd never had such a good student.

The cricket said, 'I am better. I am better. I am better.' He only lost count after ten times and then he started again.

'We'll continue tomorrow,' the sparrow chirped. 'I'll bring cake and show you how I avoid falling and how I get better without any effort at all.' He skipped around cheerfully in a little circle and then flew off.

Neither the elephant nor the cricket said a word.

THE CRICKET'S HEALING

The cricket dragged himself home in the dark. So I'm better, he thought gloomily. The sombre feeling seemed to be bashing something in half that was actually unbreakable.

The elephant stayed where he was on the ground and kept his eyes shut. I'm not going home, he thought. I'll start again first thing tomorrow morning.

But when he woke up the next morning, he heard the oak rustling in the distance and gave up on any more lessons.

41

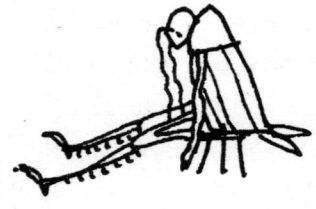

The cricket was visiting the ant. It was a bleak day.

'I have to get better, Ant,' the cricket said.

'Yes,' said the ant.

'But I'm not getting better.'

'No,' said the ant.

'I feel so sombre…'

The ant didn't say anything and the cricket let his head droop down onto his chest.

It was quiet for a long time.

'If I don't get better,' the cricket asked after a while, 'what then?'

'Then you'll become something else,' the ant said.

'What?' the cricket asked.

'I don't know what it's called,' the ant said. Her voice was hoarse and she looked very serious.

'Do you explode?' the cricket asked. The sombre

feeling was pounding the inside of his forehead with heavy objects that felt like tree trunks.

'No, you don't explode.'

'Do you start dancing?' the cricket asked. 'Gloomy dancing?' I'm just saying the first thing that pops into my head, he thought.

'No, you don't start dancing,' the ant said.

The cricket couldn't think of anything else.

They drank a small cup of tea each, as the ant's cupboards were almost empty.

They talked about embarrassing mistakes, pouring rain, and sorrow. The ant explained what sorrow was. The cricket nodded.

'That's what I've got,' he said.

It had grown late, but the cricket couldn't stand up.

'I can't any more,' he said.

The sombre feeling was big and too heavy to lift.

'Do you rip in half if you don't get better?' the cricket asked. 'Or do you dry out?'

'It's not something you can guess,' the ant said.

She explained that it was something she hadn't been able to figure out either.

'I've figured everything out, Cricket,' she said. 'But not that.'

'Is it Falling?' the cricket asked.

'Don't try to guess,' the ant said.

Then they stopped talking and fell asleep with their heads on their arms on the ant's table.

42

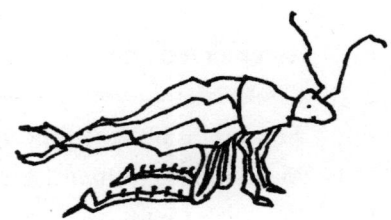

The next day the cricket went to see the longhorn beetle.

I have to get better, he thought.

In front of the longhorn's house he saw a sign saying:

> DO NOT DISTURB.
> I'M NOT HERE.
> LONGHORN BEETLE

The cricket hesitated, then knocked anyway.

'Longhorn,' he said.

A growling sound came from inside the house.

'You're disturbing me,' the longhorn said.

'I'm sombre,' the cricket said, 'so sombre...' He stepped inside.

'Oh, I see,' the longhorn said. 'I suppose you want to get better. Is that it?'

He emerged from the darkness, grabbed the cricket by a feeler and swung him around his head three times.

'Sombre, is it?' he said.

'Yes,' squeaked the cricket.

Then the longhorn beetle let go of him. The cricket smacked into a wall and sank to the ground in a crumpled heap.

'Better,' said the longhorn.

He grabbed the cricket by the nose and threw him out of the house. Then slammed the door shut.

The cricket was lying outside on the step. 'I'm better,' he groaned. He hauled himself up onto his feet and tried to jump. He couldn't manage it. But he did feel cheerful. The sombre feeling in his head was gone.

'Better!' he shouted. 'I'm better!'

Then the sombre feeling came rushing back, squeezed in, and filled the cricket's head with stamping and growling again.

I shouldn't have shouted, the cricket thought. I should have hidden. Then it wouldn't have been able to find me any more.

He sat down on the ground. Now I'm disappointed too, he thought. Sombre in my head, disappointed everywhere else.

He toppled over onto his side.

I can't go on, he thought.

But he stood up again. I have to get better, he told himself. I have to!

He looked back at the longhorn's sign. How can he not be home? he thought.

Not daring to knock again, he turned and walked into the forest, thinking, How do I get better?

Inside his head, the sombre feeling cleared its throat and said, '*That* is the question…' in a grating, mocking voice.

Don't cry, thought the cricket. Don't cry now. Have some pride.

43

That same morning the elephant went to see the longhorn beetle too. Something has to happen, he thought. Now he even had lumps on his toes, on his ears, on his trunk and on his belly. There wasn't a spot on his body he hadn't landed on at least once.

Shaking his head and with a fierce look in his eyes, he knocked over the sign in front of the longhorn's house.

The longhorn was sitting at his window and saw the elephant approaching. I see, he thought.

'I don't want to fall any more, Longhorn,' the elephant said the moment he came into the room. 'I don't want to ever fall again.'

The longhorn looked past him into the distance, where a small white cloud was hanging over the mountaintops.

'I'm sick of it,' the elephant said. 'But what's the alternative? When I climb, I always fall.'

The longhorn yawned.

'Can't you think of anything?' the elephant asked.

'Swimming,' the longhorn said. He stretched and went over to lie down on his bed. He closed his eyes.

The elephant was still standing by the door. Swimming? he thought.

'Do you mean instead of climbing?' he asked. But instead of answering, the longhorn turned over onto his side and began to snore loudly.

The elephant went back out and stood thoughtfully in front of the longhorn's door. Then he nodded, ran at top speed to the river and jumped into the water.

So it's swimming that I want to do, he thought.

With his mind made up, he swam downstream. Every time he thought it was time to climb up onto the bank, he shook his head and thought, No, I want to swim. Swimming is all I want to do. And it's true, he thought, I'm not falling any more.

Sometime after nightfall, he swam out to sea.

The next morning he was still swimming. He was very tired and he could hardly keep his head above water. But I'm not climbing, he thought, and that means I'm not falling either.

Towards midday he bumped into the whale. 'Hello, Elephant,' said the whale.

'Hello, Whale,' the elephant panted.

'What are you doing out here?' the whale asked.

'I want to swim,' said the elephant.

'Oh,' said the whale.

'I don't want to climb any more,' the elephant said. 'Do you climb sometimes?'

'No,' said the whale.

'And do you ever fall?'

'Fall?' the whale said. She thought long and hard. She wasn't entirely sure what falling was. 'No,' she said.

'See?' said the elephant.

The whale took him with her and they drank briny tea with seaweed in a remote bay where there were no trees at all. Thank goodness, thought the elephant. He told the whale all about Climbing and Falling.

'Ah…' the whale said over and over. 'How special!'

'Yes, it's really special!' the elephant exclaimed. Tears sprang to his eyes when he told her about the oak and the linden and the plane tree.

'You can stand on top of a tree,' he said.

'Really?' asked the whale.

'Yes,' said the elephant. 'You can even stand on one leg. On *one leg*, Whale…!' Then he fell silent, took another sip of tea and said, 'Well, I'll swim on now.'

THE CRICKET'S HEALING

The whale waved goodbye.

Slowly the elephant swam on to the middle of the ocean. Swimming never hurts, he thought sadly.

44

When the animals were gathered together and discussing the cricket and his sombre feeling and how he had to get better, the snail stepped forward.

'I know how to do that,' he said. 'I'm better.'

He stood on his head.

'I'm way better!'

The animals gazed at him with wide eyes and didn't say anything.

The snail fell over on his side, stood up and smashed his shell to pieces.

'Don't do that!' the animals shouted.

'Don't tell me what to do,' the snail said. 'What do I want with a shell? I'm going to stay out in the open air. I'm better, aren't I?'

He ran a short distance and smacked into the beech. It was a hard blow.

'Did you see how the beech bumped into me?' he called. 'Stupid tree...'

He laughed, fell backwards into a muddy puddle and stood up again, thought for a moment, looked up, let an enormous grin spread over his face and climbed into the beech.

'Don't!' the animals shouted again.

But the snail was already at the top of the tree, where he stood on his tentacles and fell.

Just before hitting the ground, he unfolded two black wings and flew away, slowly flapping. 'See?' he cawed.

The astonished animals watched him fly off. 'Is that what you call a miracle?' the ones who had never seen a miracle asked.

'No,' the ant said. But she didn't say what it was.

After the snail had disappeared out of sight, the ant explained that there were many kinds of 'better', just as there were many kinds of cake. The bear nodded.

'Some kinds are tart or musty,' the ant said. 'Real "better" is sweet. Like honey.'

In the distance, they could hear the snail roaring. It suddenly got dark.

'I'm eclipsing the sun!' the snail bellowed.

The animals shivered and crept closer together. The bear leant on the tortoise's shell. 'Mud pies,' he mumbled, lost in thought, 'they don't do a thing for me.'

'Sorry, I didn't catch that,' said the tortoise, who had slipped back into her shell out of embarrassment about the snail and his peculiar haste.

'And gall cake with sludge,' the bear mumbled. Far away there was a loud splash.

Soon after, they heard the snail shouting, 'Swim, River, otherwise you'll drown!'

Then it was quiet.

The hedgehog cleared his throat and said, 'Regarding the cricket…'

45

The animals' meeting lasted all night. After everyone had had their say, they all went to the cricket's house in a long procession winding through the forest.

The cricket was still in bed and staring up at the ceiling. The sombre feeling in his head was calling him names: 'Fool! Nitwit! Non-entity! You should be ashamed of yourself!'

The cricket didn't know what he was supposed to be ashamed of. Everything, probably, he thought.

The animals filed into his room.

'We've all come to do something for you, Cricket. It doesn't matter what,' said the ones at the front. 'That's what we've decided.' They shook his hand and patted him on the back.

The animals behind them squeezed their hands through so they could shake the cricket's hand and pat him on the back too.

When the room was completely full, they sang for him, blew dust off his shoulders and cleaned his feelers.

The ones who knew secrets whispered them in his ear and the ones who knew riddles told him the answers.

Some animals baked cakes, some poured sweet honey down the cricket's throat and told him he was looking very well. Other animals climbed onto his table and delivered speeches in which they called him 'esteemed' and 'most special'. Or else they shouted in his ear that he shouldn't take any of it to heart.

The cricket's house was packed and outside there were hundreds more who all wanted to do something for the cricket.

'Our turn, our turn!' they shouted.

'Soon!' shouted the animals who were inside and still doing something for the cricket.

The walls of the house creaked and fell over, while the roof got caught on the deer's antlers. The cricket didn't notice any of it because the buffalo was holding him tight and patting him encouragingly on the back.

'Ow,' said the cricket.

'Yes,' said the buffalo, 'mild encouragement is no good to anyone.'

Across from the cricket's house, the elephant climbed the plane tree and fell from the top. 'In your honour, Cricket!' he shouted, hoping that the cricket could hear him. Then he hit the ground with a thud.

New animals were still appearing. The sea lion climbed out of the river and asked, 'Where is he? What's he look like?' He wanted to tell the cricket how much he liked him. And the peacock called out that the cricket should look at him for a moment.

Now and then a cake came flying in, specially baked for the cricket in the desert or on the other side of the ocean.

Clouds slid in front of the sun and it started to rain. But nobody wanted to take cover. 'We can take cover afterwards,' the rhinoceros said. 'Getting better can't wait.'

It wasn't until hours later that everyone had done something for the cricket. 'Are you better now?' asked the animals who were closest to him.

The cricket looked up. His eyes were big and sorrowful and he didn't answer.

'Or almost better, at least?' they asked. But once again the cricket didn't say anything.

The animals saw that he wasn't better. What now? they thought, and looked at each other. Nobody knew.

Then they went back home, following each other in a long and serious procession. We did our best, they thought. Nobody can say otherwise.

The cricket's roof was still stuck on the deer's antlers and the bear was carrying an enormous willow cake on his back. He doesn't like it anyway, he thought.

On the way, they met the snail, who was looking pale and dishevelled. 'I'm upset,' he mumbled. 'I am so upset…' He didn't want to talk to anyone and crept under a bush until they were all gone.

The cricket was left behind on his back on the ground in the pouring rain. The sombre feeling in his head was swinging from side to side and wouldn't stop.

Only the squirrel had stayed with him and was trying to put his house back together. He used the floor as a roof.

It grew dark without any sign of the rain stopping.

'Finished,' said the squirrel. He picked up the cricket, carried him into his house and put him to bed.

Then he sat at the foot of the bed and waited until the cricket had gone to sleep.

46

The elephant wanted to climb the oak. But the hippopotamus was sitting on the lowest branch, leaning back and relaxing with his eyes closed.

'Could you get out of the way, please,' the elephant said.

The hippo opened one eye, saw the elephant and said, 'No.'

'But I want to get past,' said the elephant.

'I was here first,' the hippo said.

'Out of the way!' shouted the elephant.

'No,' said the hippo.

The elephant turned red, stamped on the ground, glared furiously at the hippo and raced off to the beech. But the beetle was sitting on the lowest branch of the beech and wouldn't let the elephant past. And in the linden it was the toad that was blocking his way.

'I want to climb!' the elephant yelled.

There was an animal sitting on the bottom branch of every tree. Even the pike was sitting, gasping for breath, in a tree, and a little bit further along the carp was sitting in one too. And nobody moved aside.

Finally the elephant came to the forest glade and sat down on the ground. I have to climb, he thought. I have to!

But he couldn't think straight any more.

The sun was shining and the thrush was sitting at the top of the oak. 'Thrush…' the elephant groaned.

The thrush sang a long, cheerful song, doing a little dance step every now and then or standing briefly on one leg.

Suddenly there was a peculiar sound. As if something was breaking.

It's something inside of me, thought the elephant. He didn't know what there was inside of him, and he definitely didn't know what there was inside of him that could break.

Then, in the middle of the day, in the forest glade, he climbed straight up into the sky. He had turned scarlet and the glow he was giving off was visible far into the distance.

The animals on the lowest branches of the trees pushed the leaves aside and watched him with amazement.

'You can't do that,' they cried.

'I have to,' the elephant shouted, halfway up into the sky and already far above the tops of the tallest trees.

'But…' the animals called.

Then the elephant fell. He had to fall too, he thought disconsolately.

There was an enormous crash. The whole forest shook, the earth split and the river overflowed. The elephant had never hit the ground this hard before.

The animals quickly climbed out of their trees and raced to the hole in the ground the elephant was lying in. He looked ash-grey and every part of him was broken or bent.

It was only after a long time that he opened his eyes. But he still couldn't move.

'Will you please never do that again?' he whispered when he saw the animals' faces.

'No,' the animals said. 'We'll never do it again.' And they lowered their eyes.

47

The cricket was lying on his bed staring up at the ceiling.

There was a knock on the door. The squirrel came in.

'Hello, Cricket,' he said.

'I'm not better yet,' the cricket said.

'No,' said the squirrel. He sat down on a stool next to the bed. He'd brought his lamp with him and showed it to the cricket. But the cricket shook his head. He didn't want to swing on the lamp. He didn't want anything.

The squirrel fluffed up the cricket's bed now and then, opened the window and closed it again, and asked if there was anything he could do for him. But the cricket didn't want anything.

'Isn't it time for you to go away again?' the cricket asked after a while.

'Would you like me to go?' the squirrel asked.

'No,' said the cricket.

The squirrel didn't go.

It was a cold day. Now and then they heard a loud thud in the distance and a voice calling out, 'Ow.' Otherwise it was quiet in the forest.

After sitting there at the cricket's bedside for a long time, the squirrel started to feel like he could look into the cricket's head and see the sombre feeling. It looked big and grey.

If I'm very careful, the squirrel thought, maybe I can grab it.

The cricket was lying on his back with his eyes shut. He wasn't moving. The squirrel stood up very cautiously, bent over silently, reached out with his right arm and rested one hand on the sombre feeling.

It was cold and slippery. The squirrel shuddered.

I have to grab it, he thought.

He reached out with his other arm too and carefully put his other hand on the sombre feeling as well.

Then he grabbed hold of it.

'What?' cried the cricket. 'No! Where?' He shot up.

The sombre feeling in his head was going wild, but the squirrel held on tight. He pulled and pulled. The cricket groaned and shook from side to side. The squirrel had to brace himself and was almost thrown up into the air. But he didn't let go and pulled with all his might.

Then the sombre feeling ripped. The squirrel flew backwards. But he had a big chunk of the sombre feeling in his hands. He banged down on the floor. The cricket flew backwards too and bashed into the wall next to his bed.

The squirrel stood up, showed the cold, slimy thing he was holding to the cricket and tore it into a thousand pieces, which he later stamped into the ground outside.

'It's not gone,' the cricket said when the squirrel came back in again later. 'But it is smaller.' He looked at the squirrel with a serious expression on his face.

The squirrel was still panting and sat down again.

A little later he tried to grab the rest of the sombre feeling. But it had got so small it was easy for it to hide in a dark corner of the cricket's head.

'Just leave it,' the cricket said.

When it got dark the squirrel went home.

Under the ground he heard the mole calling out, 'What's all this?'

'Sombre shreds,' the squirrel called back. 'Leave them alone!'

THE CRICKET'S HEALING

'Ah,' said the mole and she hurried off to tell the earthworm that she'd found something gloomy.

The squirrel quickly dug the pieces of sombreness back up and tore them even more until they were little bits of dust, small black flecks of dust that couldn't do any more harm. He blew them up into the air and the wind carried them off far, far away where nobody lived.

Tomorrow I'll try something new, the squirrel thought and walked on. But he didn't know what.

48

'Thinking is so beautiful, Squirrel,' the elephant said. They were sitting under the beech one summer's morning.

The squirrel nodded and thought about distance and roast beechnuts.

'Now, for instance, I'm thinking about climbing the oak. In fact, I just hoisted myself up onto the first branch.'

The squirrel didn't say anything.

'And now I'm already halfway. It's absolutely effortless!' the elephant said. He waved his trunk and jumped up onto his feet. His ears were flapping.

'Now I'm imagining I've arrived at the top of the oak. The sun's shining and I can look out over the whole forest. Hello, Thrush! Hello, Swallow! Hello, Squirrel! I'm calling you. You're a little dot. Did you know that?'

'No,' said the squirrel. He leant back comfortably and thought about roast beechnuts with honey and chestnut. He gazed at a small white cloud and licked his lips.

'Now I'm thinking that I'm not falling and I'll never fall again,' the elephant said. 'Thinking is so easy... Nothing to it!'

'No,' said the squirrel.

'And now I'm imagining that I'm standing on one leg on top of the oak and shouting out in all directions that I—'

Suddenly the elephant stopped talking. The squirrel saw deep furrows appear in his forehead as he looked around in fright.

Then the elephant screwed up his eyes and groaned softly.

'What are you thinking now?' the squirrel asked.

'Nothing,' said the elephant. He rubbed the back of his head.

The squirrel didn't ask for any more details. He pulled out a piece of sweet linden bark that he'd buried under the beech and gave it to the elephant.

'What else is there besides thinking?' the elephant asked after he'd taken a bite of the linden bark and said how delicious it was. 'I mean, what else could be so beautiful?'

But the squirrel had never heard of anything that came close.

49

The sun was high in the sky.

Am I actually shining properly? he thought. He could never be sure about it one way or the other. Sometimes he shone a little brighter, sometimes more gently. But was it right? He thought about it all day long.

At night he was always tired from shining, but mainly from thinking, and he set. Below the horizon he fell asleep immediately. He didn't have a clue what it looked like down there.

When he woke up, he would jump up, confused for a moment about where he was, then climb quickly into sight and start shining again. Then it was morning. He loved the morning. Why isn't it always morning? he often thought. He didn't understand why not.

Sometimes clouds appeared and gathered in front of him. Then he thought, What now? and scratched the back of his glowing head with his rays.

Oh, yeah, he thought after a long or short while. Appear. I have to appear, that's right. Then he crept out from behind the clouds.

In the depths below him he saw the world. He saw the desert, the forest, the river with its glittering ripples, the steppe, the sea…

He also saw little dots that sat still or moved. Sometimes they were all in one place and milling together, sometimes they flew up or disappeared under water, and sometimes one suddenly stopped.

The sun didn't know what exactly they were. Specks of dust? A kind of star?

The sun frowned. I'm not shining properly, he thought. I'm sure I'm not shining properly. But how am I supposed to shine? Who can I ask? Not the moon. She only knows questions, not answers. And shining like the moon, so pale and dented, that was something the sun would never want to do.

There was nobody he could ask.

I have to shine; he knew that for certain. But if you ask me, that's the only thing I do know, he thought. Sometimes he tried to shine differently for a change, a little fiercer, a little weaker, a little more like he was under water.

It's strange being the sun, he thought. Nobody knows how strange it is.

He glowed and shone a little brighter, a little sharper. Ah, he thought, now I'm sure to be shining just right. I have to shine like this all the time. If only I could!

The river glittered and the little dots were relaxing everywhere.

It was summer; high in the sky the sun was shining.

50

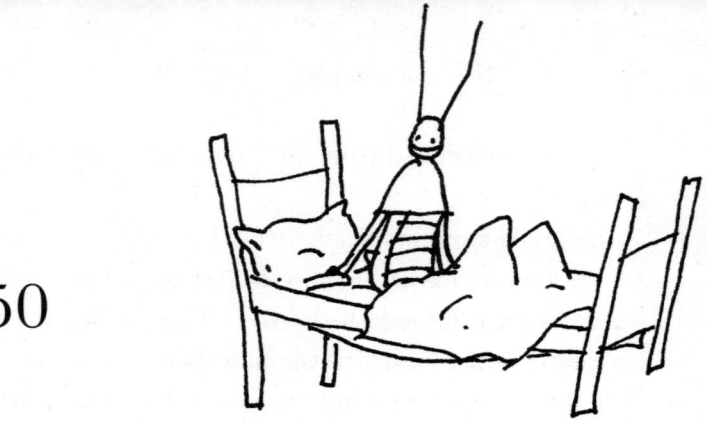

Early in the morning the cricket woke with a start. The sun was shining in through his window. Specks of dust were dancing above his table and the letters full of advice and good intentions the other animals had sent him were stuck on his walls, things like 'Sombre today, cheerful tomorrow', and 'Nobody chirps the way you chirp'.

The cricket sat up straight.

There was something strange. Something very strange. But what?

He looked around. He saw the floor, the ceiling, the door, the cupboard, the table, the chairs and the window. Everything was just like always.

His curtains fluttered gently in the morning breeze.

Then he realised.

The sombre feeling in his head was gone. His head was empty. Thoughts emerged timidly from chinks and

THE CRICKET'S HEALING

gaps and shot awkwardly through the newly empty space.

It's gone! thought the cricket.

He looked around again. Could it be hidden somewhere? Very cautiously he looked under his bed, in his cupboard, under his table and up the sleeves of his green coat. But the sombre feeling was gone. It had disappeared without a trace.

He jumped onto his table. 'Hungry!' he cried. 'I'm hungry!' He grabbed an enormous jar of willow sugar out of the cupboard and ate it all in one go.

Then he shouted, 'Chirp!' He sat down in front of his door and started chirping.

Everywhere in the forest the animals pricked up their ears.

'Who's that chirping?' they asked each other. 'The cricket? The sombre cricket?'

The cricket chirped loudly, wildly, for hours on end.

The animals streamed in from near and far to listen to him.

At the end of the morning he got hungry again and stopped chirping. For a moment his thoughts turned to the sombre feeling. He hoped it hadn't crept into somebody else's head.

He fetched a jar of thistle honey out of his cupboard, ate it in three mouthfuls and climbed onto his roof. He looked around and said, 'I'm better.'

'Why?' asked the bug, but the cricket didn't hear him because all the other animals were cheering.

When they'd finished, the rhino cleared his throat and asked, 'How did you get better?'

Everyone looked expectantly at the cricket.

The cricket hesitated for a moment and bent over to the ant, who was among the animals at the front. 'How did I actually get better?' he asked softly.

'Just like that,' the ant whispered back. 'Say that. It's easiest.'

'Just like that,' the cricket said. 'I just got better.'

He jumped up, spread his wings and flew down to the ground from his roof. 'And I'll never be sombre again!' he cried. He waved his feelers and his eyes sparkled.

The sky was blue and standing at the top of the oak was the elephant, grey and glowing in the morning light. He heard what the cricket had shouted, turned a half turn, saw the cricket at the bottom of the linden and called, 'And I'm never going to—'

The rest of his words were lost in the rustling of leaves, the snapping of branches and the warm sunshine.

51

It was winter. The animals were sitting under the oak in the middle of the forest, packed in close. They were eating warm honey and beechnut pie and wearing thick coats and hats.

They were all cheerful and satisfied. When they got cold, they slapped each other on the back or blew on each other's hands and wings.

The ant was next to the cricket and began to ask, 'That sombre feeling…'

'Which sombre feeling?' the cricket asked.

'The sombre feeling you had in your head…'

The cricket frowned and thought deeply, but he couldn't remember having had a sombre feeling in his head. 'Did I have that?' he asked.

The ant looked at the ground and didn't say anything.

THE CRICKET'S HEALING

The wind rose and the animals moved even closer together. A letter from the penguin floated down, saying that he would love to come too, but it had to snow first.

The sky was thick and grey.

The ant stood up, cleared her throat and asked if anyone remembered anything.

Silence fell. The wind died down again.

Remembering... thought the animals. Remembering... Nobody knew what it was.

'Is it a sound perhaps?' the frog asked.

'Is it something slow?' asked the snail.

The ant explained what remembering was. But when the animals asked what it was good for, she could only shrug.

'I don't know,' she said. 'Maybe nothing.'

The animals wrapped their arms and wings around each other again and stopped thinking. A couple of them stood up and started to dance.

The ant looked at the ground.

Memories swirled around her in thick clouds.

She remembered distance, the ocean, the birthdays of rare animals, long conversations with the squirrel, summer...

Summer... she thought.

The cricket jumped up. 'I don't know why,' he chirped, 'but I am very cheerful.'

The animals clapped their hands and wings.

The elephant stood up and looked up at the top of the oak, which was dark and veiled by cloud. No, he thought. No. He sat down again, but immediately jumped back up onto his feet and looked up again.

That was how the animals sat there in the middle of the forest under the oak on a cold winter's day. And while the cricket chirped cheerfully and the elephant looked up and sighed, the ant walked off unnoticed, into the darkness.

It started to snow. Thick snowflakes swirled down and stuck where they landed: on the dark earth, on the bare branches of the trees, on the bushes, on the undergrowth, and on the animals' heads and shoulders.

Memories swarmed around the ant, stinging her neck and eyes. I have to go, she thought and walked out of the forest and across the frozen river to the other side, where she disappeared in the distance.